"You're crazy,

Charlotte's words we
onto balconies at 6:0

Bobby gently massag
Romeo worth his salt would do the same." With
an appreciative look downward he added,
"Although I doubt many Juliets are as exciting
on waking as you are."

She pulled at the sheet, but he laughed softly and
tugged it away. "This is crazy, Bobby,"
Charlotte said with no real conviction. "We're
late as it is . . . ."

He only bent closer, until his lips were a breath
from hers. "Lady . . . hush." His hands cupped
her breasts, his touch both soothing and
arousing. "We do have time—forever. At least
as long as that."

The Sky's the Limit

JILL BLOOM

MILLS & BOON LIMITED
ETON HOUSE, 18-24 PARADISE ROAD
RICHMOND, SURREY TW9 1SR

NORTH
AMERICA

EUROPE

AFRICA

SOUTH
AMERICA

1.
2.
3.
4.
5.
6.

Charlie and Bobby traveled 4620 miles short of a complete equatorial circumference of the globe.

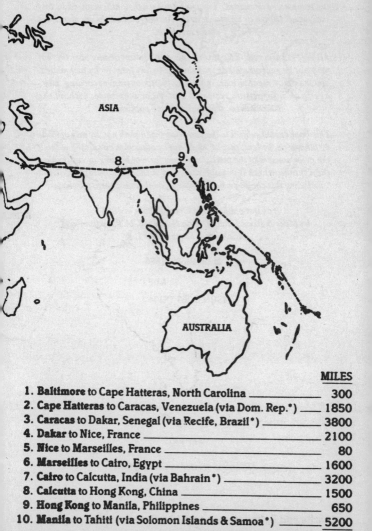

	MILES
1. **Baltimore** to **Cape Hatteras, North Carolina**	300
2. **Cape Hatteras** to **Caracas, Venezuela** (via Dom. Rep.*)	1850
3. **Caracas** to **Dakar, Senegal** (via Recife, Brazil*)	3800
4. **Dakar** to **Nice, France**	2100
5. **Nice** to **Marseilles, France**	80
6. **Marseilles** to **Cairo, Egypt**	1600
7. **Cairo** to **Calcutta, India** (via Bahrain*)	3200
8. **Calcutta** to **Hong Kong, China**	1500
9. **Hong Kong** to **Manila, Philippines**	650
10. **Manila** to **Tahiti** (via Solomon Islands & Samoa*)	5200

Total Miles Traveled 20,280

*First published in Great Britain in 1993
by Mills & Boon Limited, Eton House, 18-24 Paradise Road,
Richmond, Surrey TW9 1SR*

© Jill Bloom 1986

ISBN 0 263 78194 1

21 - 9303

Made and printed in Great Britain

1

"WELL, WHAT DID YOU THINK?"

"Think about what?" Charlotte Frehling, Charlie to her friends, looked up from her copy of *Flying* magazine with an absentminded smile.

Marla Evert sighed with exaggerated patience for her employer's benefit. "Think about what? We're in a clothing store, remember? One of the four stores you own, as a matter of fact. And we just came from an important buyers' show—what do you think I'm talking about, the latest thing in jet propellers?"

Charlie grinned and put the magazine down on her desk. "Jets don't have propellers, but I get your drift. Consider my wrists slapped."

Marla grinned back, easily mollified. "Your wrists must be sore from so much slapping these days," she commented lightly, perching on the edge of Charlie's desk. "So let's start this conversation over. What did you think?"

Charlie ran her hand back through her thick waist-length hair and gave a little tug on the clip that held the honey-brown mass high off her neck in a chignon. This was a characteristic gesture that meant she was giving the question some serious thought while buying enough time to switch her mind off the article on turbo-charged combustion engines she had just been reading. "What did I think?" Now her mind's eye could easily visualize the show they had been to that morning as well as the parade of sportswear as if it were, at that very moment, passing down the runway in front of her. "Well, to tell you the truth, Marla—" Charlie pursed her lips "—I wasn't all that impressed."

"I was afraid of that," Marla said with a slight grimace. "What didn't you like about the fashions?"

"Well, for one thing, I didn't like the colors. Those primaries are last year's news—I'm ready for something a little softer—something unusual."

Marla rolled her eyes. "So what else is new?"

Charlie ignored this, now absorbed in the subject at hand. "And the fabric wasn't right, either—too stiff or too tightly woven or something—I don't know. It just didn't sit right in my gut—know what I mean?"

Marla nodded forbearingly. "I know, I know. If your gut doesn't say it's right, it isn't right." The two women exchanged smiles. Charlie's gut reactions were an old joke between them, since she was one of the most knowledgeable professionals in the sportswear business. But although Charlie tended to downplay her expertise and go with her instincts, she was seldom wrong about a fashion trend. Marla, as her executive assistant, had been with Charlie long enough to know this.

"The question is," she asked her boss, "what are we going to do now? We've got to start buying for the fall and winter lines—all four shop managers are clamoring for merchandise. They say all their competitors are already advertising next season's lines, and they want to know what you've got up your sleeves."

"Good! Let them wait!" Charlie's violet-gray eyes sparked a brighter shade of amethyst when she got angry or excited; she was both now. "They know me well enough to realize I'm not going to be content to show what all the other stores on the block are showing—and they should be glad! Think of the excitement that builds when you're the last to unveil something new. Let all the other folks make the fashion mistakes. We're going to do something really special this winter!"

She leaned forward eagerly in her chair. Then, just as suddenly, she let her head fall back against the dove-gray tweed headrest, and the sparkle in her eyes died to a ruminative gleam. "The question," she murmured, more to herself than to Marla, "is not when, but *what*." She glanced idly around at the apricot-colored walls of her office, which took up the back half of the flagship branch of Electra, her sportswear boutique in downtown Baltimore. She had intentionally created a soft and unimposing atmosphere so that her imagination would be free to wander without visual distractions.

But after her eyes had roamed the subtle tones and soothing textures around the room, they came to rest on the copy of *Flying* magazine that lay open on her desk where she had left it. When she looked up at Marla again the sparkle was back with a vengeance. "What fashion concept? An excellent question," she went on with a wicked chuckle. "And I've just decided exactly how to answer it."

Marla looked at Charlie, looked down at the magazine, then back up. "Uh-oh," she said, rolling her eyes, "I think I know what you've got in mind."

"Bet you don't," Charlie challenged.

Marla sighed. "You want to do more jumpsuits. More parachute material and more aviation-inspired styles like that satin bomber jacket that was such a big hit last year, right? Another flight theme."

"Yes, no and no," Charlie replied promptly. "Marl, you don't honestly believe I'd do something twice, do you?

Those bomber jackets are already outmoded, and so is the parachute material."

"They may be," Marla pointed out, "but those styles are still selling out in all the stores. The managers can't keep enough of them in stock."

"I know, I know. That's because it was such a terrific idea." Charlie flashed a satisfied grin. "I knew millions of women feel like I do about sportswear—that if it isn't easy to get into, easy to wear and easy to take care of, then it isn't really sportswear. It's some man's idea of how a woman ought to look. But—" she held up a long finger and waved it around in the air "—that doesn't mean I can't take a good idea and make it better, does it?"

Marla would have replied affirmatively to this rhetorical question, but she didn't get a chance to open her mouth.

"Of course I can! And that's exactly what I'm going to do. Only we're going to have to do a little more traveling in the next month or so to make it work."

"More traveling? Three trips to Europe and one to Japan weren't enough?"

"Nope. Not nearly enough. Or rather, we haven't been going to the right places. Paris, London and Tokyo aren't the only places in the world where fashion statements are being made, you know."

"There's New York and Rome," Marla murmured, but she wasn't heard.

"No, what I have in mind means trips to some very out-of-the-way places—places that have never heard of *Vogue*." Charlie leaned forward again and took Marla's hand. "What do you think of this? We'll do our basic jumpsuit style and all the variations, but we won't use the old industrial aeronautic-type fabrics we used last time. Instead we'll go to places like Bali and Dakar and

South America and the Pyrenees and find lovely native fabrics, exotic prints and tiny florals, deep-toned cottons and delicate paisleys, all the kinds of cloth you would least expect to see in a jumpsuit. We'll make our jumpsuits glow with color, drape like silken saris, burst with vibrant prints. And it will still be that same perfect-for-everything style that women seem to love so much!" She squeezed Marla's hand in her excitement. "Well, what do you think?"

Marla smiled and shook her head. "As usual, Charlie Frehling, you've managed to take an utterly impractical idea and make it sound marvelous. Of course it will work!" She returned the hand squeeze with pleasure, and then her smile changed to one of amusement. "Of course, I suppose this means more traveling in the company plane."

"Of course!" Charlie released Marla's hand and sat back with a triumphant smile. "Not only does it mean more travel, it means traveling in the best sense of the word. It means," she added with undisguised glee, "that I'm going to be doing some fancy flying in the near future."

"I wondered when you were going to work that into your schedule."

Charlie looked up at her and shrugged, feigning innocence. "Well, that *is* why I bought the plane, isn't it? I do far too much traveling for the Electra shops to bother with commercial flights. We have the shops in Nice and Caracas, not to mention this one and the one in New York. Between my shop-hopping and my buying trips, a plane is a necessity."

Marla looked as if she had heard this all before, which she had. "And I suppose your commercial pilot's license was a must, too," she mused. "After all, why bother with charter planes when you can spend hundreds of hours worrying over flight plans, weather conditions, carburetors...." She broke off. "As if you don't have too much to do in your life already, Charlie."

Charlie recognized the gentle remonstrance in Marla's voice; she had heard it before. "I know, I know," she said soothingly. "It does seem like an awful risk to you, Marla. And I know it makes for a lot of extra work for—for both of us, since I'm so caught up in the technical aspects of our traveling. But it's not too much for me, really. I *need* to fly, Marla—it's what I've wanted to do all my life. You know that. For me, all the excitement of flying, the freedom of being able to soar up there over the clouds with only the sun for company—that's the most wonderful relaxing experience. You know that's why I bought the plane. It's what I live for. Or what I would live for if I could afford to," she added wistfully

Marla's expression softened at this emotional outburst. "I know, dear," she said, smiling wistfully. "I just wish I wasn't such a chicken so I could accompany you on your airborne adventures. It does sound enticing when you talk about it."

"I'm going to do it someday," Charlie promised impulsively. "I'm going to get you over your fear of small planes."

"Oh, no, thank you." Marla pulled back and raised her hands protectively. "Your idea of helping me overcome a fear is probably to get me up there and then make me take the wheel."

"It's not a wheel, it's a stick," Charlie informed her with a giggle. "And it's called a yoke, for your information."

"Whatever. I know how you operate, Charlie, and I'd rather sit back in a huge jumbo jet and pretend I'm taking the bus. Up there in that tiny tin box . . . ugh!" She shuddered, and Charlie laughed.

"Okay, okay, don't panic. Nobody's going to force you up there." She reached across the desk for the magazine. "No, what I've got planned is not for the faint of heart, much as I'd like to have you along for the ride."

Marla took one look at her employer's face and grew suspicious. "What exactly do you have up your sleeve, Charlie Frehling?" She tried to get a glimpse of the magazine, but the print was upside down. "There's something in that issue that ties in with this new notion for the fall line, isn't there? You've got some scheme worked out already, haven't you?" Charlie's eyes, wide with feigned innocence, confirmed her fears. "Come on. Out with it. What are you plotting?"

"Read it for yourself," Charlie replied, and pushed the magazine back to Marla, who read the copy on the page with growing amazement. Watching her, Charlie became more and more animated. "Doesn't it sound exciting? Don't you think it would be incredible?"

Marla looked up. "Incredible? I think it sounds suicidal! Charlie, you can't be serious!"

"Of course I can. Why not?" Now Charlie's innocence was genuine. She read the words in the magazine aloud as if trying to find out what was so objectionable.

Eighth annual circumnavigation of the globe contest. Open to all class 1 business jets, with or without payload, Cape Hatteras to Hawaii with stops in Caracas, Dakar, Marseilles, Bahrain, Cairo, Calcutta, Hong Kong, Manila, Hawaii. Pilot and copilot only, plus two-man ground crew provided by the Fédération Aéronautique Internationale and its representatives in all host countries. Times and distances calibrated by the American and French branches of the International Aviation Federation. Sponsored by the trade commissions of said port cities. Departure date, June 1, 1986.

"What's so suicidal about that?" she asked.

"It's . . . you just can't, that's all," Marla concluded lamely.

"Well, why not?" Charlie bounded out of her chair and began pacing the room. Although she was of medium height, her long legs and athletic build, along with the forward thrust of her body as she moved restlessly around the room, gave her a forceful presence. She filled the entire space with her energy. Strands of hair came loose, and several times she reached up to tug at the scrimshawed ivory clip. Marla watched as her boss talked and paced. Charlie was remarkably catlike at that moment, sleek and healthy, sinuous, but adept at lightning-quick changes in direction. Right now she was speaking very rapidly, another telltale sign of excitement, and her eyes were burning a deep purple, the color of anemones on a bright spring day.

"Really, Marla, why not? The list of pit stops sounds like an ideal shopping itinerary to me—Dakar, Bahrain, Cairo. . . . Just think, Marl, of all the fabulous materials we could pick up! And I have that great manufacturing connection in Manila, so I could just drop off the samples of what I've bought on my way through there and show them what I want done with the materials. We could easily get the bulk fabric and the finished stuff shipped through—I'd get my shopping and my production taken care of in one trip. And I would have the time of my life. Really, the contest is tailor-made for me." Charlie grinned. "All puns intended."

She paused in her travels for a brief dazzling smile, and Marla tried to respond, but it was useless to try to interrupt at this point.

"All I need to do is let Jim Sullivan out at the airfield know about my plans so he can get *Electra* ready for the trip. Then I have to check with the international aviation people and see if I can get them to make a few changes in the flight plans for me. And I'll have to get myself a good copilot, because I know Jim won't be free to fly with me on something like this. And of course I'll have to get all the patterns cut and finished before I leave so I can drop them off in Manila with the fabric samples—do you think our pattern cutters can get a dozen patterns in ten sizes out by next month?" Charlie didn't stop to hear the answer but gave Marla a squeeze on the shoulder. "Oh, Marla, this is going to be the best winter collection we've ever had, I just know it. Isn't it a marvelous idea?"

"The idea for the collection is wonderful," Marla replied carefully, "but as far as I'm concerned this around-the-world contest sounds dangerous. What if something happened to you, Charlie?"

"Oh, what could happen?" Charlie placed both hands on Marla's narrow shoulders and brought her face close to her assistant's, willing the doubts away with her eyes. "I'm an excellent pilot, and I've got .ny instrument rating, you know. Besides, I'm sure Jim Sullivan can recommend someone good for my copilot. There will be trained ground crews in every port to check *Electra*, and every move we make will be watched by the FAI. Anyway, this isn't exactly the search for the Temple of Doom, you know, Marla. They've been running this race for eight years, and we're not landing on virgin airstrips in the jungle. These are well-equipped areas they're talking about." She paused and looked up, her eyes focused on some faraway vision. "And what places! Bahrain, India, Egypt . . . what colors, what sights, what fabrics!"

Marla smiled. "I suppose it could work," she conceded, having discovered that objections would go unheeded.

"You suppose? Of course it will work! The timing is right, the route is right...." She turned suddenly and took Marla's hands in hers. "And I have you to watch things here at home for me. I know I couldn't do any of this madness without you." Her expression grew warm and gentle. "And you know I've been wanting to do something like this all my life, Marla. It may be madness to you, but it's so right for me."

Marla chuckled. "Okay, okay. As long as you know that some people in this world call it madness, you may as well go ahead with this crazy plan. And of course you don't have to worry about me here. I can handle this end of the business."

Charlie gave Marla a hug hard enough to almost send her sprawling. "Oh, Marla, I knew I could count on your blessing!"

Marla had to laugh outright at the absurdity of this statement. "As if you need my blessing—the idea! I know you, Charlie, and I know you won't rest until you do this. So I might as well give in and agree to help you out, right? After all, we've got a lot of work to do to get ready for this . . . this circumnavigation of the globe, haven't we?"

Immediately Charlie straightened up, pulling Marla with her. "You're absolutely right," she said, resuming her most businesslike tone. "And I suppose we'd better get right back to work, wouldn't you agree?" She resumed her seat, leaned back and picked up a pencil, which she drummed absently on the table as she thought.

Marla barely had time to straighten her blouse and pick up a notepad before Charlie began to rattle off details.

"Let's see...we've got to get those patterns ready, and I should call Jim right away to see about the plane. And if you would, Marla, please schedule me time out at the airfield to interview prospective copilots. That's going to be a very important position, and I want to be sure I have the perfect person for the job...."

CHARLIE WAS RIGHT about the amount of work she had to do. Planning a buying trip was one thing, but planning such a trip to the out-of-the-way corners of the world was another matter entirely. That, along with the fact that the trip was to be combined with an air race, made the next few weeks seem impossibly full of meetings, scheduling sessions and general hubbub. Charlie was constantly on the phone to retail brokers around the world, trying to buy fabric and clothing she had seen on previous buying trips, booking factory time so that the fabric she collected could be made at short notice into her winter line. Marla was given the task of sorting through the patterns Charlie had approved and getting them made up in all sizes so that they, too, would be ready in Manila as soon as the bulk fabric arrived by airfreight. Charlie's small staff worked overtime to untangle the intricate web of import laws, customs laws, foreign production laws and tax laws. At the same time her assistant buyer ran herself ragged securing the required accessories such as buttons, zippers and trim while placing orders with wholesale houses for those few other sportswear lines that Charlie would allow to be sold in her shops.

The whole process was madness, but no one who worked for Electra Boutiques, Inc. expected anything less. They all knew the story of Charlotte Frehling's rise to success, a story that had, in the six years since Charlie had been in business, focused a great deal of attention on the young businesswoman. After graduating from a New York City school of design, Charlie had spent five years working for a major designer, first as an accessory buyer, then as a junior designer. The head designer had taken quite a shine to Charlie, enough of a shine, some said, to make her his lover as well as his protégée. Charlie had long since stopped trying to deny this untrue aspect of her professional history, having learned that people were too eager to believe gossip to pay the least attention to her denials.

She had left the designer when it had become clear that she would always be standing in his shadow—and when she had decided that she enjoyed the retail end of the business more than the wholesale. The designer, angry at the defection of such an asset, had predicted an early demise, especially when Charlie had opted to open her first tiny store in downtown Baltimore rather than New York. The young professionals in that smaller city had had a special flair that matched Charlie's slightly off-beat approach to fashion, and customers had flocked to her little corner shop.

Two years later, when the time had come for her to think about expanding, Charlie had pulled another surprise. On a buying trip to France, she had decided that Europeans wanted to see some funky American fashions in their stores, just as Americans had wanted to see European styles. So she had opened her second store in Nice on the French Riviera. It, too, was an immediate success. People in the fashion world began to watch the idiosyncratic young Charlotte Frehling. Charlie liked the attention. She appeared at fashion shows wearing eye-catching white cotton caftans over tight black capri pants, or her signature parachute jumpsuits, lightly flowered gauze shirtwaists that looked vaguely antique but were in fact extremely daring, worn over a full body stocking.

It wasn't until Charlie had opened a third store in Caracas that she had bowed to pressure and the inevitable, opening her New York boutique in SoHo, below Greenwich Village. This quickly became her most successful branch, but Charlie chose to keep the Baltimore store as her home base. The city, she insisted, had a certain streetwise charm, and that was where she got her best ideas—on the streets.

At thirty-two, Charlie no longer dressed to make a daring statement about her business. She had settled into a personal style that reflected her firm belief in comfort as well as fashion. In addition to the casual and elegant jumpsuits that had become Electra's trademark, Charlie favored slacks cut to order in exquisite thick linens and cotton and big, easy tops that hung like sculptures on her strong, spare frame. The one thing she had never changed was her hair, which she still often wore straight down the middle of her back like a shiny waterfall. A long fringe of asymmetrical bangs framed her face and accented her remarkable lavender eyes. Her makeup was understated, leaving a smattering of pale freckles visible across her longish nose. Her one concession to high chic was her penchant for long, lacquered fingernails.

Today they were painted a deep fuchsia, and they were drumming impatiently on her knee as she listened to her old friend, Jim Sullivan, talking common sense. "I know, Jim, I know. It takes people like that a long time to make a decision. But I've got to get on with my plans, don't I? I mean, the American officials of the FAI have already agreed that *Electra* comes in under the requirements set forth in the race bylaws. I can carry a small payload. They understand that I'm not going to use the trip as a tax write-off, since all my own funds are paying for *Electra*, so that I can conduct my business. So why are they so uptight about the fact that I'm carrying real cargo instead of the fake weight called for in the race requirements? What difference should it make to them if I carry bolts of fabric instead of bales of cotton batting, as long as I stay within my weight allowance? Why are they giving me such a hard time?"

Again she listened as Jim, who was the operator of the airfield where the company plane was hangared, tried to get her to understand that these things took time, that officials often needed a lot of prodding to deviate even slightly from their orders. Jim Sullivan was convincing, but Charlie was not comforted in the least. She wanted to know that everything was going according to her plan. The unnecessary delays were making her impatient and nervous. She almost wished the FAI would give her a firm "no," rather than stringing her along for weeks. At least that way she would have something to fight against. It was the waiting that she hated.

But she didn't wait idly. Aside from the long business meetings in her store offices, she visited Jim Sullivan's airfield every day, spending hours watching as he went over the updated Lear jet, checking it out for the trip. As he worked, Jim would give her pointers about the trip—what kind of flying conditions she could expect in different parts of the world, how to handle them, what the airstrips were like and what Charlie might expect in some of the countries.

Jim Sullivan had been an air force reconnaissance flyer in World War II and had returned to Baltimore to set up his own flight school. He had been the only flight school operator to agree to give Charlie private lessons, in spite of the fact that he could have made a good living as her charter pilot. Jim had seen the delight and determination in Charlie's eyes the first time she had taken the controls of *Electra*, and he had given her nothing but encouragement during those difficult early days.

Even after she got her license, Jim still acted as Charlie's copilot on her transatlantic flights. But as Charlie flew more business trips, Jim's airfield business grew more successful and time-consuming. Lately she had had to hire copilots on a one-time basis when Jim wasn't available.

They had already discussed the possibility of his accompanying her on this trip but had reluctantly ruled it out. The question was who else would do? The few suitable pilots were either unavailable or involved with their own plans. And there were too many candidates that Charlie had to rule out.

"I need someone flexible," she said to Jim. "Someone who understands that I'm in charge on this flight, but who can take over when I have business to attend to. Someone who's strong mechanically, because that's my weak spot, but who can put up with my style of flying."

Jim looked up from the wheel he was checking and grinned. "You mean someone who can sit still while you turn off the automatic radar controls and fly by the seat of your pants, don't you?"

Charlie grinned back. "That's what I had in mind, yes."

"'Fraid not, Charlie. No hotdogging on this trip. You may have made the New York to Nice run a hundred times and think you can do it in your sleep, but no pilot can ever afford to be too confident about their flying, certainly not when they're flying in unaccustomed airspace. There are some pretty tricky currents up there over the equator, and out in the Pacific there's no emergency landing field if you track a few degrees off course." He leaned his head out from beneath the wheel base. "You have to promise me that you'll fly by the book for this race, Charlie. No one's good enough to take any risks on this course—believe me, I've been there. You've got that instrument rating—I want you to use it. Is it a promise?"

Charlie smiled saucily, but she spoke sincerely. "It's a promise. Anyway, I wouldn't want to give these officials any reason to pull me from the lineup. It's bad enough that I'm a female pilot, and that I'm asking for special considerations before we even take off. I know they would just love to disqualify me and get me out of their hair."

Jim chuckled. "That's because they don't know you yet."

"You're right. But they're learning . . . they're learning." The two of them grinned conspiratorially. "And you have to promise me you'll help me find a decent copilot, agreed?"

"Agreed."

Charlie left the airfield that day feeling extremely confident, but arrangements didn't prove that easy to work out. She interviewed a few possible candidates for the job, but the few who seemed eager were clearly not qualified. The ones who were didn't seem comfortable at the prospect of working for a woman and on Charlie's terms. Charlie suspected the lack of candidates was a sign of the inherent sexism in the aviation industry. No pilot worth his license would want to drop his plans to charge around the equator as second banana to a woman. The few men to whom gender wouldn't matter were usually in charge of their own planes, or they were charter pilots who earned a good living on lucrative short hauls in big planes, men who had no interest in Charlie's relatively low pay scale.

By the time the plane was ready and the last-minute details for the patterns and fabric settled, Charlie still hadn't come up with a copilot. Only two weeks remained before the first competitors were scheduled to depart, so that Charlie was edgier than ever. Jim had helped her out as much as he could. He had even found a dozen possible candidates by advertising in *Flying* magazine, although he admitted he didn't know any of them personally or by reputation.

"You're just going to have to play it by ear with this bunch," he told Charlie one afternoon. "Do you want me there with you to check these guys out?"

"No, thanks, Jim. You've spent far too much time on my problems as it is. Besides, I'll be able to tell what will work for me, and they all have résumés I can check. I'll have Marla schedule them at fifteen-minute intervals out at the airfield this afternoon, and we'll just hope for the best."

"Fifteen minutes each? Do you think that's long enough?"

Charlie smiled. "Actually, I'll have made up my mind in the first five minutes, but nobody would believe I could make a real decision that quickly, so I'll have to let them hang around an extra ten."

"That's true," said Marla, who had come into the office at the tail end of the conversation. "As a matter of fact, given two sportswear lines of equal merit, Charlie could probably make up her mind in five seconds rather than five minutes—and she'd be uncannily right, too."

"But since we're dealing with people and not pant-suits, I guess I'll have to give these guys the benefit of the doubt, right, Jim?"

"I think it might be generous of you," Jim said dryly, and they all laughed. "Still I'm curious, Charlie. What are you looking for in a copilot besides the basic skills?"

Charlie thought for a moment. "I'm looking for someone I can trust completely," she said carefully. "Someone who understands what I'm doing and why I'm doing it and agrees that it's worth all the work I expect of him or her. Someone who doesn't have to be told what to do and what not to do for me. Someone who can finish my thoughts for me before I've finished them myself." She looked up and shrugged her shoulders. "Now that's not too much to ask, is it, Jim?"

"Too much? Oh, no, of course not." He laughed. "It's only asking for the perfect mate—it's only asking for the world. Where do you expect to find this paragon?"

Charlie turned her eyes toward Marla and said mischievously, "I already have. Marla here is my perfect copilot. Why, she thinks my thoughts before I do sometimes! She'd be the perfect candidate for the job."

Charlie was clearly joking, yet Marla shuddered. "Except for the fact that I get faint at the mere thought of going up there in the wild blue yonder without a thousand tons of steel between me and the air, I'd be a great choice." She shook her head. "Oh, Charlie, if only you'd picked a nice safe earthbound obsession, like cross-country skiing, or knitting, I would have been happy to join you. But up there in those paper airplanes—never!" Marla's eyes flashed with unaccustomed fervor. "Not even for you, Charlie."

Charlie and Jim exchanged glances and amused shrugs. It was hard to believe someone could actually dislike what they loved so much. "Well," Charlie said with a rueful smile, "I guess that's that, then. It's all up to those interviews this afternoon. If I don't find the perfect copilot then, the trip's off."

CHARLIE DROVE OUT to the airfield later that afternoon, praying she would find what she was looking for by the time she was through with the interviews. She had gotten a lot of work done at the shop that day, and she felt her energy buoying her up for the ordeal. She would find the right person—or a reasonable facsimile. She wasn't going to let the race slip through her fingers; her threat to cancel the trip had been an idle one. It meant too much to her to stop now, even if her final plans hadn't yet been approved by the FAI.

As she drove she thought about the first time she had been bitten by the flying bug. When the need for a company plane had become apparent, Charlie had bought the older Lear jet because she had loved the lines and because the previous owner had ingeniously updated it. Charlie had arranged for Jim to be her charter pilot even before she'd bought the plane, yet had been content to sit in the eight-seat passenger section in front of the cargo bay, delighted to be gazing out at the ever-changing sky while being ferried from one shop to another.

One afternoon Jim had called her into the cockpit and had told her to take the controls, "just for the fun of it."

Charlie had been in the copilot's seat many times before, to chat with Jim or to gaze out over the silver nose of the trim jet at the vast blue sky that opened up before her. But she had never taken the controls and so had never given the mechanics of flying her total attention. Now it seemed as if a whole new dimension of space were confronting her, and she trembled with excitement as she felt *Electra* responding to her touch. "Hey! This is really terrific!"

"You're pretty good," Jim said in his characteristically lazy voice. "You should consider learning to fly this bucket o' bolts."

"You mean it?" Charlie's eyes shone with such pleasure that even the taciturn Jim had to smile.

"'Course I mean it. If you can run a business, you can run a little scattershot like *Electra* here. Nothing to it."

Of course that had been an understatement. There was plenty to it, and Charlie, once she started on a project, was not the type to abandon it or do it less than thoroughly. She spent hours each day at the airfield, in classes and up in the air. Marla convinced her to let her take over the everyday functions of the Electra shops, but Charlie took over all the paperwork duties and ordering chores, so that she was often up until way past midnight poring over her work. For the first time in her life she looked unhealthy. Her leanness turned to boniness, and her pallor was highlighted by dark circles beneath her eyes.

As soon as she got up in the air that all changed. Her face took on a flushed, rosy glow, her eyes sparkled, and her entire body radiated energy.

"Yup," Jim had said back then, watching her peer endlessly into the horizon as if she owned it, "a natural-born flyer is what you are."

She got her pilot's license in record time, then went on to get her commercial-class certification. It was a tremendous feat for Charlie, logging those endless hours of flight time required by the stringent licensing board. But she never wavered in her determination. Two years ago she had made her first solo flight from Baltimore to New York, carrying thirty dozen dresses and a case of champagne to share with the friends who awaited her at the other end of the line.

She hadn't made a transatlantic crossing until the following year, and then always with a crew to back her up. The circumnavigation race would be the first time she would handle *Electra* with a light crew, but Charlie didn't fear the outcome. She felt as if her entire life had been a preparation for this journey and, indeed, the idea of flying around the world had been a dream since early childhood, although she had never imagined she might be piloting the plane herself!

All of which brought her back to thoughts of a copilot. She pulled her tiny M.G. into the airstrip parking lot and got out. Smoothing her gray cotton jumpsuit over her hips, she made her way across the wide stretch of tarmac to Hangar B, where *Electra* was parked. The afternoon was golden and quiet with promise, and Charlie approached the corrugated tan dome with barely controlled excitement. It wasn't just the prospect of meeting her future copilot that made her heart beat faster—she felt this way every time she saw *Electra*.

Ignoring the narrow office in which Jim had arranged for her to interview the prospective candidates, Charlie undid the heavy combination lock and with tremendous effort pushed back the huge door to the main hangar. Inside, the light filtered down from the thirty-foot roof in long golden shafts, and Charlie's gray lizard heels echoed through the quiet, vast room.

There were a half dozen small planes in Hangar B, but Charlie only had eyes for *Electra*, sitting in the far corner in a particularly brilliant shaft of sunlight. Her fuselage was all white with touches of silver around the

nose cone and wings, set off by smart navy blue letter-
ing and trim. She sat at a pert angle to the cool cement
floor, as if she would spring into the air at the slightest
provocation.

By the time Charlie had been ready to procure a plane
for her business, she had known enough about small jets
to know the Lear jet was considered obsolete. Still, ever
since she had begun to look at glossy pictures of light
planes she had thought the Lear line had surpassed all
others in terms of sheer physical beauty and economy of
design. Despite her aerodynamic thrust, *Electra* looked
as if she had no angles, only curves. Her wings spread out
low and sleek from her fuselage like plummage. *Electra*
was a smooth, neat bird of flight, a female bird of flight.

Everyone always assumed Charlie had named *Electra*
after her chain of stores. Few people knew she had named
her stores after a plane—Amelia Earhart's plane, to be
exact. Amelia Earhart had been Charlie's heroine ever
since she could remember, and no one, not even Marla,
knew that behind Charlie's determination to complete
the circumnavigation of the globe was a desire to finish
off that tragic flight of 1937, which had begun in a twin-
engine Lockheed Electra. A sound from the office behind her interrupted Charlie's reverie, and she turned to
see the silhouettes of several people against the dusty
glass. She glanced at her watch and realized it was time
for the interviews to begin.

"Okay, honey," she said, running her hand across the
smooth underbelly of the plane in a parting caress. "Here
goes nothing. Wish me luck."

Charlie stepped into the office. The walls were lined
with green leather chairs, old government-issue models
with straight backs and tubular steel legs. About ten of
them were occupied by men ranging in age from early

twenties to late fifties. They were dressed in everything from three-piece suits to old flight jackets and jeans, but there was clearly a camaraderie among them, an intimacy to their low-pitched chatter, which stopped abruptly when they saw Charlie.

She knew as she scanned their expectant but guarded faces that they were watching her as closely as she was watching them. She advanced slowly down the length of the long, narrow room, her steps falling with precision on the gray-and-green linoleum. At the far end of the office was a small enclosed cubicle with a desk and two more chairs. The walls were covered with outdated aviation maps, the windows with generations of cigarette smoke. Hancock Field had been used by the air force during World War II, and it still carried the ambience of that era in its cinder block walls.

As she walked, it occurred to Charlie that some of these men might have seen action during the war, might have sat in this very room to confer. In deference to their experience, she felt a generous impulse toward the older men, but the impulse was stanched when she caught one of them raising an eloquently condescending eyebrow to another as she passed by. *Well*, she told herself, *that scotches that guy's chance for glory*.

She waited until she had reached the door to the inner office before she turned to face the men. "My name," she began without welcoming preamble, "is Charlotte Frehling. I intend to enter the eighth annual circumnavigation of the world contest being sponsored by the FAI. The race begins two weeks from yesterday, so the person I hire should expect to begin work immediately to organize our plans and get the plane ready. I fly a 1977 model Lear Jet II turbo with custom interior and a twelve thousand cubic-foot payload bay." She saw a smile flicker across someone's face at the mention of the customized interior. "That doesn't mean I have fluffy pink carpeting and poodles on the walls, gentlemen. My idea of a custom turbo is microwave radar, computerized navigational equipment and the latest specifications for maximum auxiliary fuel capacity. Gentlemen, this is not your average Lear jet."

Charlie allowed herself the smallest smile when she saw the expressions on some faces. She rattled off another series of technical terms and watched the expressions change from disbelief to grudging admiration. Only a few men remained impassive during her short speech. Those, she decided, would be the ones worth talking to.

She settled herself behind the scarred oak desk in the inner office and began seeing the applicants one by one. As Marla had predicted, it was an effort for Charlie to drag the interviews out for a full fifteen minutes. Within a few moments she could tell if the candidate would be suitable. They all had adequate training and more than adequate experience, but most of them clearly thought flying around the world—especially with a woman at the helm—was a harebrained scheme.

In fact, it was hard for her to figure out why some of them had bothered to apply for the job at all. Certainly not for the pay, because she couldn't afford to offer the huge sums that a purely commercial venture would. The prize money was minimal, too, although she had offered to share that. And there was less glory in being a hired copilot than there was in piloting one's own plane.

She had to assume the men were here because they were curious, because they were unable to find other work, or because, when it came to the more promising applicants, they were so smitten with the idea of flight that they didn't consider reward or glory in their decision to apply for the job. Of the three reasons, only the last carried any weight with Charlie; all other things being equal, she set out to look for diehard flyers among her applicants.

Unfortunately, she couldn't find it in any of them. Certainly a few seemed to have some spark of interest in their eyes, and one or two looked genuinely interested in what Charlie was doing, as opposed to looking interested in what she was wearing, but no one candidate gave her that feeling of rightness that accompanied all good decisions, whether "gut" or "considered." "I wish Marla weren't afraid of everything above the third story," she muttered to herself about midway through interviewing the candidates. "I wish there was one woman out there. Then, at least, there would be a fighting chance of being on the same wavelength." She thought about Marla's uncanny ability to finish Charlie's thoughts for her. That was what she wanted in a copilot—an alter ego.

When the last man got up to leave after a mere eight minutes—during which Charlie couldn't help stifling a yawn—she was barely able to smile and tell him she would be in touch in a few days. It seemed useless to even bother calling any of these men back; none of them was remotely suitable as company on a two week journey in a four-by-six cockpit. Charlie was disappointed. She had come to this interviewing session so full of high hopes, but she knew she couldn't compromise on her choice. A copilot was more than a technical assistant. He or she was another pair of eyes and ears, another heartbeat up there in the blue vastness of heaven, another soul to fly with. Just anybody wouldn't do.

Charlie sat at the big desk for a long while after the last person had left the hangar. The light was fading, and the sun streamed softly through the old panes at an oblique angle that gave the impression of golden liquid pouring down from a glass pitcher onto the cement floor. She could just see *Electra* through the glass that separated the office from the hangar; the plane was half in shadow, half in that honey light. Charlie sighed. Maybe some other applicants would turn up tomorrow. Otherwise maybe she *would* have to settle for one of the men she'd seen today.

After staring vacantly at *Electra* for a few moments, she smiled slowly, brightening. She got up and went into the main hangar, where from a corner cupboard she took a pair of faded blue overalls and a handful of tools. With a big grin she turned to face *Electra*. "Okay, sister, let's have some fun."

Charlie jumped onto the wing step on the pilot's side and unhooked the forward doorway. The plane's interior was dark and cool. She didn't bother to switch on any lights as she walked toward the cockpit. She knew her way blindfolded around every inch of *Electra*, inside and out. Slipping down between the two pilots' seats and turning on her back, she then slid beneath the control panels. Anyone who had seen her face as it disappeared from view would have thought she had won a million dollars.

Charlie wasn't an expert on the inner workings of *Electra*'s complex mechanical and technical instrument panel. But what she had learned, aside from the basics required of every solo pilot, she had learned from long sessions doing just what she was doing right now. One by one she was taking apart the delicate instruments on *Electra*'s instrument panel and putting them back together after examining and analyzing each component until she was sure she understood exactly how it worked.

Usually she had Jim Sullivan or one of his flight mechanics with her, just in case she couldn't do what she had undone, but this evening she felt the need to involve herself totally in the project and take the consequences of any mistakes later on.

Although Charlie adored the excitement of running her business and was proud of her accomplishments in choosing creative clothing for women, nothing gave her quite as much pleasure as *Electra*. She loved flying her, but when that was impossible, she enjoyed tinkering with her almost as much. In a way this was even more relaxing than flying, because then Charlie had to be alert to so many things at once. This way she could focus her concentration on one very small aspect of the plane and drown out whatever other problems were plaguing her.

Right now the problem of a copilot—or, rather, the lack of a copilot—was pushed to the back of her mind, since she'd become engrossed in disassembling the altimeter, spring by tiny spring. As a matter of fact, she was so absorbed that she didn't hear her name the first time it was called.

"Miss Frehling?"

No reply.

"Miss Frehling? Charlotte?"

The second time she was so startled by the proximity of the voice that she banged her head hard against the instrument panel in her panic to get upright.

"Ouch!" She squeezed out from under the steel plate and rubbed her head with her hand. It took her a moment to adjust her eyes, so that the figure who stood over her in the cockpit was just a shadow. "Who in the hell are you and what are you doing in my plane?" she demanded.

The man, who had been bending over at what must have been an uncomfortable angle for someone so tall, slipped into one of the pilot seats with a single graceful sweep of limbs. Now that his face was nearer, Charlie could see he was smiling.

"You *must* be Charlie Frehling. You're just like they said you'd be."

"Like who said I'd be?" Charlie was now too absorbed in rubbing the rising bump on her forehead to take issue with a perfect stranger making himself at home in her plane—and in her seat, not the copilot's. There would be time to read him the riot act when the spots cleared from her vision.

"The guys you just interviewed. If you could call those interviews." The man chuckled, and Charlie caught his Southern accent more clearly in his slightly drawled speech.

"What the hell do you mean by that?" she demanded, forgetting about the bump on her head in her annoyance.

The man shrugged. "The guys I met on my way in here. As they were leaving, I could hear them talking about you. Helluva looker, one of 'em said. But he added that he'd sooner work for a cobra than sit in a cockpit next to you." He chuckled again, then stopped when he saw the look on Charlie's face. "Of course, none of them mentioned the fact that you're probably as good a pilot as any of them—that would be asking too much of those guys." He squinted and scanned the cockpit as if one of "those guys" might possibly be lurking in the minuscule area.

His eyes, Charlie noticed, were deep-set and golden brown and surrounded by very thick lashes. But she wasn't in any mood to concentrate on them at the moment. "Really?" she said in her chilliest voice. "And how is it that *you* know what a fabulous pilot I am?"

He shrugged again as if this was as clear as day. "No one but a dedicated pilot would spend an hour underneath an instrument panel getting intimately acquainted with her altimeter if she didn't care a whole lot about flying." He paused for a beat to watch Charlie's face soften. "Besides," he added almost shyly, "I got the word about you from Jim Sullivan. He told me to come over here."

A moment ago there would have been nothing in the world to make Charlie even consider the man before her as a candidate for the job—she assumed that was why he was here—but the name Jim Sullivan worked wonders. If Jim had sent this guy, there must be something to recommend him, although she couldn't imagine what that something might be—certainly not his toast-and-honey eyes.

"So," she said, playing for time until she could lift herself into a more dignified position in the seat beside him, "Jim sent you, huh? Why did he think you'd be right for the job?"

The dark eyes gazed at her steadily. "Because he knows I'm as crazy about planes as you are," he said simply.

Now that they were on an equal level, it was easier for Charlie to assess the man opposite her, and she could tell he was taking a moment to do the same thing. He was very tall, as she had seen earlier, and lanky, although not without attractive muscular ripples beneath the sleeves of his pale blue polo shirt. His hair was light brown, a shiny light brown with blond highlights that she could see even in the penumbra of *Electra*'s cockpit. It was slightly long and obviously not styled, and the sight of several dangling strands behind his ears hinted that he probably did his own trimming. The effect was rather appealing.

He had a longish, delicately formed face with a surprisingly strong jaw and wide mouth. His nose was thin and chiseled but clearly overshadowed by his luminous eyes with their heavy brows and lashes. They reminded Charlie of beacons, so completely did they infuse his face with light. They were lighter than either his hair or his deeply tanned skin.

"Why. . . why didn't you show up for the interview?" she asked, trying to sound stern and unimpressed but having to clear her throat before she could speak. His simple statement of commitment to flying had impressed her.

"I was here. I came to see *Electra* first." He saw her eyes widen, and he smiled slightly. She noticed a slight crookedness to his front teeth. "It was important to me to see what I'd be flying. I'm a mechanic before I'm a pilot, which is why Jim thought I'd be good for the job. That's why I had to take a look around—to see if the airplane and I were right for each other. If not—" he shrugged eloquently "—it wouldn't have worked."

"You were here all the while that I was in here? Why didn't you make yourself known right away?" Charlie asked. She was uncomfortable with the notion that he might have been watching her while she was unaware of him, but his comment about the setup being "right" echoed her own thoughts on the subject.

He shook his head slightly as if to dispel her unspoken discomfort. "I didn't see you come in. I've been out back checking the tail fin rudders and the braking system." In spite of his obvious effort to maintain professional distance, a smile lit up his face. "It's a honey of a plane you've got here, Charlotte Frehling."

Charlie couldn't help but smile in response. "I couldn't agree with you more," she said warmly, and for a moment the two of them gazed at each other, acknowledging their common bond of respect for the plane in which they sat.

"Of course," he added after a moment, "I don't know what you're going to do about that altimeter you just ravaged there." He nodded down at the floor between them, and Charlie, following his gaze, saw the scattered springs, coils and dials she had just extracted from the heart of the instrument panel.

"I know what I'm doing," she said, though her tone lacked conviction. The confusion of tiny parts was alarming, and her train of thought had been interrupted. She doubted that she would know how to put the altimeter back together.

"Well, let's see." He dropped on his knees between the two chairs and bent down to rummage among the parts. Charlie looked at the strong ridges of muscle beneath the cotton knit shirt. She was silent for a moment.

"I know what I'm doing," she finally repeated, but at the same moment she got on her knees beside him, unable to resist the pull of her curiosity. "Which way does the tension spring go in?" she asked, leaning over to watch as his long brown fingers worked.

"Normally it goes in this way," he said, "the way you were doing it." He gave her a brief look of approval, then turned back to the work in his hands. "But I've been working on a way to reverse the tension, so that the dial responds much more sensitively. You could conceivably get the same exactness with this baby as you do on your computerized altimeter, if you modify it this way."

Charlie nodded silently, her eyes riveted on his fingers, which were working with lightning speed on the delicate parts spread between them. He had long, rather pale hands, more suited, she thought, to piano playing than flying. Yet as he worked, she realized he was an artist in what he did. This had probably been the reason Jim Sullivan had sent this man to her. Her considerable talents as a pilot would be more than matched by this man's magic with the mechanics of a plane. Jim had more than met Charlie's need, and she sent a silent thank-you to her absent mentor.

But she still wasn't ready to hire this stranger—not only did she want to check him out more closely with Jim, but she had other less tangible qualifications in mind as well. This man may have been an ace mechanic, but somehow Charlie felt he was not the alter ego she had been hoping for.

Still, he did work magic with his hands, and for the next hour while she watched him work on *Electra*, she forgot all about her mission to hire a copilot. After the altimeter they attacked the brake cable—it seemed he had ideas about improving that as well. Then he took a look at her computerized equipment, and after protesting that he knew very little about it, proceeded to take it apart and put it back together so that it worked like a charm.

By the time they emerged from the cockpit onto the floor of the hangar, it was dark. Only a yellow work light was on in the cavernous domed building; they moved automatically toward the golden glow. This was the first time Charlie had walked beside him, and she was impressed once more by his immense height. Yet he seemed not to have been bothered by all the ducking and bending. It was almost as if the interior of a plane was his natural habitat.

Charlie looked up at him out of the corner of her eye. In profile, with the yellow light illuminating his features, he was really quite handsome. It was interesting that in the plane she had been more taken with his skills than with his looks. She usually had an excellent eye for physical harmony. Then she chided herself for being chauvinistic. After all, men evaluated her physical attributes all too often, and she didn't appreciate that one bit.

Still, it was nice that he was handsome, though inconsequential. If one intended to spend two weeks in the cockpit of a small plane with a stranger, trying to carry out a challenging and sometimes dangerous task, one did not consider physical attributes. There was no time to consider them; one would then be in danger of losing the very skills that made a good competitor in the first place—concentration and control.

They had reached the door leading to the office on the side of the hangar. To prove that she wasn't intimidated by the man, Charlie slipped out of her overalls as if she did that sort of thing all the time in a man's presence. If he appreciated—or even noticed—her svelte figure in the gray jumpsuit underneath, he didn't acknowledge it with his expression.

"So," he said, leaning against the dusty windows and turning his eyes back to where *Electra* was highlighted by the moonlight flooding the hangar, "do I get the job?"

Charlie considered. He had been late for the interview —really, he hadn't shown up. But that had been because he had wanted to meet *Electra* before he met her. There was no other excuse she would have accepted. If he was sincere about the job, his approach was the best recommendation he could have offered. If he had discerned that his words were what she would have wanted to hear, then he could read her like a book, and that was a pretty good recommendation in itself.

She adjusted the collar of her jumpsuit and looked up at him. "I don't know the first thing about you," she said, not really believing that herself.

"You know Jim recommends me. Or should I say you know that I claim that he recommends me." Again he shrugged, and Charlie thought how young he looked when he made that gesture. How old was he? "Anyway," he went on, "you do know how I feel about your plane. And you know I can probably handle anything that could possibly go wrong with her." He smiled slightly, and she decided his smile was very grown-up. "I think that's a lot to know about a person." The smile broadened while, for the first time, his gaze dropped to her body. "It's more than I know about you," he pointed out.

Charlie decided to ignore this remark, as well as the appreciative expression in his eyes as they traveled over her body. His list of reasons was accurate, his manner relaxed, so that she returned his smile, albeit tentatively. "You're a good mechanic," she said, smiling even more at this obvious understatement, "but can you fly?"

He was almost laughing now, and there was something else in his expression that suggested he was seeing Charlie for the first time. This was definitely not the way a prospective employee should look at his employer. Charlie looked briefly away. When she looked back, only a smile lingered on his lips. "Name the time, and I'll take you up for a spin," he said.

Now they were both smiling broadly at each other, because they both knew the outcome of the conversation.

"I don't even know your name," she murmured, surprised at the heat in her cheeks. Surprised, too, that she had chosen this moment to finally ask the question.

She got the feeling that he wanted to reach out and touch her cheeks; his sensitive hands were actually trembling slightly. He checked the gesture. "My name," he said, staring into her eyes as if he were falling, "is Bobby Dupree."

Charlie found herself locked in his gaze. "Well, Mr. Bobby Dupree," she heard herself say, a signal of her acceptance, "welcome aboard."

3

WITH BOBBY INSTALLED as her copilot, Charlie found that preparations for the trip moved along a lot more efficiently. She was free to concentrate on the last-minute business details as well as the official race preparations without having to worry about whether the trip was actually going to come to pass. Having a copilot at last meant that the only obstacle left in her path was the FAI itself; the agency was still reluctant to bend the rules a bit to accommodate Charlie's business—but she had never doubted her ability to overcome *that* minor obstacle.

It also helped to know that *Electra* was in such good hands. Bobby would be able to tackle whatever mechanical changes or additions had to be made to meet the rigorous demands of lengthy flights and unfamiliar weather patterns. Besides, she had seen enough of his handiwork during their first interview to know he would do a superb job without costing her an arm and a leg.

According to the regulations stipulated by the race officials and the advice of her own company lawyers, Charlie would have to pay for all the expenses out of her own pocket—this on top of the cost of business travel for the Electra shops. She was fairly secure financially, but equipping the plane, paying the entrance fees and all the travel costs, not to mention Bobby's salary, was going to take more money than she had to spare. The only way to make the trip worthwhile was to see to it that her buying trip was spectacularly successful. The line would already be coming out late by industry standards. It was early June, and she had plenty to show for her fall line. But she knew she would have to have merchandise in the stores by early September, at the latest, for the winter collection.

Everything depended on her ability to buy the fabrics she wanted at decent prices, then get the samples to Manila to show the manufacturers exactly what she wanted done. The factory would also have to produce quality work on a strict schedule. Charlie knew that if she didn't make her deadline into Manila, the factory wouldn't be obligated to honor her contracts, and she would lose the gamble. She was used to gambling, though, and she didn't doubt that if she got the goods, she would be able to transport them to the overseas factory in time to guarantee the product. It was all up to her, but she had long since realized that self-confidence was her greatest commodity in the cutthroat sportswear business.

The key, of course, was to have someone with her who could be entrusted with the details of running the race while she went off occasionally to buy fabrics and generally manage her business. She felt in her gut that Bobby Dupree was the person to rely on.

Not that she trusted her instincts alone. She was careful to check out Bobby's résumé, which was nothing more than a sheet of paper containing a short list of handwritten job references. At first Charlie was taken aback—there seemed to be very little flight experience in his history, and the only references were to technicians' jobs. But everyone she called said that Mr. Dupree was a skilled mechanic and technician, and that he had always handled himself well in test-flight situations.

Her most important resource was Jim Sullivan, who gave Bobby a glowing if somewhat cryptic assessment. "I don't know the man well," he said to Charlie one afternoon when she dropped by after work to see how *Electra* was doing, "but I know that he's got magic in his hands when he works on a plane. There's not much that can go wrong that Bobby Dupree can't handle."

"What about his flying experience?"

Jim shrugged. "Couldn't tell you much about that," he admitted, "except that he worked for Bolton Aviation, testing out their new supersonics way back when no one in their right mind would go up there in one of those little things. He did one transatlantic hop, which is no small potatoes in an experimental jet like that, and then he left Bolton. You can see from his résumé that he's been around."

Charlie consulted the worn sheet of paper in her hand. "Yes, he never stayed anywhere for very long. And there's nothing on here before Bolton, which was only six or seven years ago." She looked up. "What do you suppose he did before that?"

Jim gave her a sharp glance. "Beats me," he said after a short pause. "I guess you'll have to ask him that yourself."

Charlie smiled. "I have a feeling he's not going to give me his life history unless it's absolutely necessary. He seems to hold his own counsel—not unlike you, Jim."

Jim grinned crookedly. "Maybe that's why I trust the guy," he replied. "He doesn't spill his guts—just says what he needs to to get by."

"That's hardly a recommendation for a round-the-world colleague," Charlie pointed out. She hadn't changed her mind about Bobby's suitability, but she found herself playing devil's advocate with Jim, trying to see what she could get him to reveal about the enigmatic Bobby Dupree.

"I don't know." Jim raised an eyebrow and pursed his lips. "A man like that might be exactly what you need. After all, familiarity has been known to breed contempt, and you're going to be in awfully tight quarters for awfully long stretches of time."

"*Electra*'s not that small," Charlie said quickly. "And, besides, we've got the whole universe to ourselves up there—you can't get claustrophobic in the cockpit of a plane like *Electra*!"

Again Jim grinned. "Bobby Dupree feels the same way you do, Charlie. That's why he's the perfect copilot for you, and you know it. Can you imagine anybody else who's more at home in a plane?"

Charlie recalled the loving hands that Bobby had laid on *Electra*'s control panel that first night, and she smiled at the memory. He had treated the plane almost like a living creature. She was about to agree with Jim when she heard a voice behind her.

"Who's more at home in a plane?"

Jim and Charlie turned to see Bobby standing in the doorway. He was wearing a pair of oil-stained overalls that, on his lean frame, managed to look appealing and almost elegant. His hair was dishevelled and falling into one eye, which he remedied with a careless toss of his head. "Who's more at home in a plane than whom?"

Charlie wondered at the grammatically correct but slightly formal-sounding "whom." He hadn't struck her as the college type, but one didn't usually pick up such niceties along with a high school diploma. Still, his honey-coated Southern drawl was pleasant, and she found herself smiling at the question. "We were wondering how you came by your natural affinity for cockpits," she told him as he came into Jim's office and straddled a narrow wooden chair.

Bobby quickly looked up at Jim, who gazed at him impassively through a haze of cigar smoke. Then he shrugged. "Naturally, I guess." As if eager to change the subject, he leaned over the back of the chair and tossed something into Charlie's lap.

"What's this?" She quickly picked up the small round object so that it wouldn't stain her pale pink jumpsuit. "A natural compass?"

"Yup. You need a new one."

Charlie looked at the greasy disc in her hand. The needle was stiff and silent as she lifted it, the compass points yellowed with age. "This came from *Electra*? I didn't even know she had one of these things."

"She does, but that one is useless. Whoever rebuilt *Electra* probably just installed the new equipment right over this, figuring no one would have any use for the old compass."

"But why do we need it? We have all that computerized equipment. I've been flying *Electra* for years, and I've never seen the need for a nautical compass."

Bobby smiled slightly but not in a patronizing way. It was as if he had expected exactly that answer. "You may never need it," he said, "but there may be times when you want it. Anyway, it's a small item, and it doesn't cost much—get a new one and I'll install it in the same out-of-the-way place where the old one was. Believe me—you may be glad you did."

Charlie looked automatically at Jim, who was nodding his head. "He's right. You never know when one of those things may come in handy." The two men exchanged small smiles of understanding, and for a moment, Charlie felt faintly left out of their male camaraderie.

Then Bobby turned to her and moved on to another topic. "How's our status with the FAI, chief?"

She couldn't help but smile at his form of address. If he had consciously planned to say the one thing that would instantly put her at ease again, he couldn't have done better than that one casual word, "chief." It was said without sarcasm, and when he looked at her with those clear eyes of liquid amber she knew she need never worry about a conflict between the sexes where he was concerned. For Bobby Dupree, she thought, the important thing was that Charlie loved to fly, and that she owned *Electra*. *Electra* was what he wanted; that was why he was there.

"Things are moving along," she told him. "I've still got to wait for final approval to land at Nice instead of Marseilles, but I've told the officials I'm willing to take a time penalty, and they seemed to be satisfied with that."

"A time penalty? Why?"

"I told you—I have business to do in Nice, and it's important that I get there. That's part of the reason for this trip, don't forget. I do have to think about my shops."

"Oh, yes, the shops." For a moment the candid eyes were hooded, and Charlie wondered if he really had forgotten her dual purpose. "Well, a time penalty—that's nothing," Bobby said easily. "*Electra* can handle a slight handicap. The important thing is that they give us clearance."

"Right. And you don't have to worry about that. I can handle the race officials."

He smiled—a warm intimate smile. "Oh, I never doubted that. You can handle them all."

Charlie smiled back. She was glad he understood her abilities as well as she understood his. They would work very well together.

"But you *have* forgotten one thing," Bobby told her, still smiling.

"What's that?"

"You haven't seen me fly yet."

"That's true, I haven't. And I should. I really should." They were watching each other, both of them teasing, enjoying the understanding beneath their casual conversation. But they shared something more than understanding—a hint of something more intense, although Charlie wasn't sure yet what it was, and she wasn't particularly comfortable with the sensation, either. She and Bobby didn't just understand each other—they seemed to be getting to *know* each other in a way that, after such a brief acquaintance, was almost scary. But she didn't scare easily. Neither, it seemed, did Bobby Dupree.

"Well," he said, "you're the boss. Give me the word, and I'll be glad to take you up for a spin. *Electra's* been dying to get out of the hangar, anyway. She's really feeling her oats."

"I'll bet." Charlie chuckled at the image of *Electra*, sleek and perky, chomping on the wooden stops that impeded her forward motion. Bobby was right. *Electra* did look as if she might take off at the slightest provocation. "Well, how about tomorrow afternoon? I'll be finished at the shop at around five. We could meet out here after that."

"I'll come by for you," Bobby said quickly. "I want to see what you've got going down there in those boutiques of yours."

He spoke evenly, but Charlie was aware of a new undercurrent. If he picked her up at the shop, the outing would seem more like a social occasion than a business-like meeting. Also, she wasn't sure how she felt about Bobby poking around the silky rows of sportswear hanging along the shop's mirrored walls. It was hard to imagine him as comfortable in that Electra as he was in the one with wings.

Still, she could hardly refuse. "All right, I'll see you at the shop at five. You know where it is?"

"Don't worry. I'll find it." Bobby still held her gaze with his, so that both of them were startled when Jim cleared his throat.

"Well, I'm glad that's settled," he said, dry humor in his voice. "Now if you two don't mind getting out of here, I do have a business to run, remember?"

They stood up hastily and said their goodbyes. Charlie waited until Bobby had disappeared back toward the hangars before she left to go back to the office. And for some reason she found it difficult to meet Jim's eyes.

CHARLIE HATED TO ADMIT IT, even to herself, but it was hard for her to concentrate on the series of meetings she had scheduled for the following day. For the first time since she had begun to plan the around-the-world trip, she couldn't see her professional life and her aeronautic life as part of a seamless whole, oriented toward the same goal. The idea of Bobby coming into the shop and watching her work amid the yards of silks and tweeds that screamed of femininity made her unaccountably nervous.

It had never occurred to her before that the atmosphere in the Electra shops might be at odds with that at Hancock Field. She had always felt perfectly at home moving between the two worlds, equally comfortable with fashion designs and flight plans. Her two loves had always seemed perfectly complementary, and the idea of combining them for the race had struck her as the perfect culmination of years of work at both endeavors.

Now there was an additional factor in the equation— Bobby Dupree. Charlie hadn't expected her choice of copilot to affect her attitude about the race at all. Yet Bobby Dupree wasn't just any copilot. By her own choice, Charlie had looked for someone who would share her own feelings about flying, and she had found him, never thinking he might clash with the other half of her life—the fashion half. Was he really the right partner for this business/competition venture?

She told herself he was, that her nervousness as the day progressed had no sound basis. Bobby had been interested in seeing the Electra boutique, so there was no reason why he shouldn't. After all, he was going to be a partner in a business venture as well as a sporting event. The more he understood about Charlie's business, the easier it would be for her to conduct it en route.

But somehow she couldn't imagine him out of the hangar and out of his copilot role. Was it reasonable to think a man like Bobby could appreciate the other side of Charlie's life, the glamorous fashion side? More importantly, why should she care what he thought?

This was the question that bothered her most. When he was working on *Electra*, Bobby held a magical attraction for her. He fit in so perfectly with her plans for the plane that she could hardly imagine ever having done without him. They were perfectly at ease together. But now she recalled Jim Sullivan's words: familiarity did sometimes breed contempt. She wouldn't only be seeing Bobby as he masterfully molded *Electra* into a perfect flying machine. She would be seeing him early in the morning and late at night, in good weather and in bad, during the easy moments as well as the tough. She would be eating her meals with him and she would be going through customs with him. There must be more to Bobby than the magical technician. She would be living with a man for all those weeks. And she was afraid the man might not live up to her expectations.

The flight would tell her a lot, of course. If he handled himself as well off the ground as he did on, she wouldn't worry so much.

In fact, she needn't have worried at all as far as Bobby and the boutique were concerned. She was in her office, looking over the final contracts her lawyers had drawn up for the manufacturer in Manila, when Marla came in.

"Charlie," she said in her crisp businesslike voice, "there's a man outside who says he has an appointment with you." Marla winked. "But he doesn't look like a business appointment, if you ask me."

Charlie glanced at her watch, knowing Marla could only be referring to one person. "Bobby's here already? But it's only 4:40! He's early, and I absolutely have to go through these contracts before I leave." She looked at Marla for help, although she realized Marla couldn't possibly know of her unaccountable reluctance to have Bobby in the shop.

"I'll just tell him to wait," her assistant said easily, watching Charlie's face closely. "Anyway, I don't know why you're worried, Charlie. The guy has made himself quite at home already, believe me."

Charlie had a vision of Bobby in the familiar overalls, sprawling on one of her satin love seats with his endlessly long legs sticking out into the narrow aisles, tripping up her customers one by one. "Oh, Lord, maybe you should ask him to come back here. I'll never be able to finish if he's in here...."

"Charlie." Perplexed, Marla shook her head. "What are you getting so excited about? Who is this guy, anyway?"

Charlie sighed. "He's my new copilot."

Marla's eyes bulged. "You're new—" Suddenly she began to laugh. "Him? I don't believe it."

"Why not?" Now Charlie was beginning to get agitated. "He happens to be the best in the business."

Marla chuckled. "He also happens to be a pretty good salesman, too. He just got some perfect stranger to buy that nine-hundred-dollar lynx cape you bought last year. You know, the one we never thought we'd be able to sell?"

"You're kidding."

"Come on out and see for yourself."

Charlie followed Marla to the front of the store. There, sure enough, was Bobby, lounging across the sales desk very close to a tall, thin woman with short blond hair.

"I'm telling you, ma'am, as soon as you walked in here I thought this beautiful piece of fluff could only belong to you."

"Did you really?" The woman paused in the middle of writing a check and looked up at him with shining eyes. "It's very expensive. My husband will tell me it's a crime to spend so much money on one thing." She made a face, but Charlie quickly assessed the woman's outfit and recognized someone who made a habit of such crimes.

"It would be more of a crime if you didn't buy it, I can promise you that," Bobby assured her. Then, turning around, he saw Charlie. "Oh, Charlie, hi! I hope you didn't hurry out here on my account. I'm having a fine time in this store of yours! You've got some great stuff!"

He looked stunning. He was wearing a pair of well-fitting khaki chinos and a pale pink sport shirt that did justice to his golden coloring. His hair was slightly damp and slicked back rakishly, revealing the chiseled lines of his tanned face to great advantage. He looked more like a tennis pro than a pilot, and he was apparently very much at ease in *both* Electras.

"I'm glad you like it," Charlie said as he bowed gallantly to the departing customer and came back to where Charlie stood. "Hopefully, after our trip, we'll have even more great stuff." She looked at him quizzically as he reached out and fingered a silk robe with a practiced touch. His success in selling the lynx cape, which had been languishing in the store since last winter, surprised her, but no more so than the fact that he was obviously at home among such luxuries. "I'm wondering," she said at last, "if I should give you a commission on that cape. That was quite a sales job—and in May, no less. Nobody buys furs in May."

"They do if the fur is meant for them." Bobby turned from his inspection of the robe and smiled at her with his warm eyes. "It's like anything else, Charlie. When it's right, you know it."

Charlie smiled back. "Of course it helps if there's someone like you around to convince whoever it is that it's right."

"You didn't need any convincing that I was the right guy for this piloting job, did you?" The smile was suddenly gone, and his warm eyes became smoky. Charlie blinked, then looked away.

"No," she said, trying to maintain her nonchalance in the face of his inexplicable intensity. He seemed to have divined her private second thoughts about him, and she was ashamed of her paranoia now. "I guess I usually make up my mind pretty quickly," she told him with a grin.

"So do I, Charlie. So do I. And like you I'm usually right the first time." Noting her astonished expression, he laughed and took her arm. "Now why don't you finish up whatever it was you had to do. I believe you and I have a date with the blue beyond, right?"

The intimate mood was broken so quickly that Charlie wondered if she had been mistaken. Maybe he hadn't divined her skepticism about him. She went back to her office and signed the contracts quickly, half her attention on the muted sounds drifting back from the shop. What was Bobby Dupree going to do next? Sell the antique mirrors in her showroom?

She finished her work and handed the contracts to Marla, letting Bobby take her by the arm and propel her out the door.

If his behavior in the shop had been surprising, the car he led her to was exactly what she might have expected from him. It was a beat-up old sedan filled with tools and other paraphernalia. Charlie remembered the quick succession of jobs Bobby had held in the past, and she imagined he had developed an itinerant life-style wandering from airfield to aeronautics factory, then leaving when the spirit moved him. She didn't even know where he was living at the moment, which wasn't important. In another week they would be taking off to rendezvous at Cape Hatteras, where the North American race contestants would officially start. From then on their home would be the sky.

It was a perfect evening for flying. The sky was clear and blue, dusted with pink in the west, where the sun was beginning to head toward the horizon. There was a light easterly wind and not a cloud in sight. Charlie and Bobby got to the hangar and, after filing their plans, boarded *Electra* and prepared to taxi out to the runway.

Bobby sat in the pilot's seat. Since this flight was ostensibly to see how he handled *Electra*, Charlie was content to let him give the directions. He expertly eased the plane out of the hangar and maneuvered her onto the longest runway on Hancock Field. *Electra* was the biggest plane at the airfield, which mostly catered to tiny Pipers and Cessnas. She needed a relatively long takeoff run, so Bobby motored her slowly out to the far end of the strip, where the low sea grass dipped neatly away from the rush of air from the plane.

He checked with the tower and got the signal. Charlie, who was watching him closely, thought she saw him tighten his jaw and swallow deeply as he throttled up to gain speed. He couldn't be nervous, she thought—he'd done this hundreds of times before. Perhaps he was just concentrating on the task. After all, he had never taken *Electra* up before, and Charlie refrained from giving him any pointers, preferring to watch him figure out *Electra*'s idiosyncrasies on his own. No, she decided, he wasn't nervous—just very, very intense.

It was obvious by the time they had cleared the ground and were banking into their flight pattern, that he was a natural flyer. All planes had their quirks; *Electra* was no exception. Even a thorough understanding of the plane's mechanics couldn't have prepared him for the fact that she lifted slightly to the right in a certain head wind, or that the throttle tended to stick at first, or that the visor window tended to warp slightly on the port side. But he found all these things and automatically adjusted to them, tripping switches and flicking levers while he gradually evened her out and brought her up to cruising height and speed.

All the while he remained silent, his brow furrowed, his eyes intent on the sky in front of him. He was so silent that Charlie began to get uncomfortable. Jim had said he was a man of few words, but she wondered for the first time if Bobby Dupree might have something to hide behind that wall of silence. He had no reason to be worried about his flying ability, that much was clear. Maybe she was wrong and had misread him completely. Perhaps there was something wrong with the plane.

"Is everything okay?" she asked warily. "*Electra*'s flying fine, isn't she?"

He didn't turn to answer her right away, but when he did the change was phenomenal. All signs of tension seemed to have been erased from his expression, and he grinned with pure delight. "Okay? Why shouldn't everything be okay? Everything's terrific! She's as perfect as I thought she'd be!" He dipped the wing of the plane in a little dance of pleasure.

Charlie watched, unsettled by his sudden change of mood. Now she was quite sure of what she had seen. Bobby *had* been nervous about something. But she couldn't deny that he was no longer the least bit upset. He was doing a terrific job of handling *Electra*. "Okay," she said slowly. "I just thought...I thought maybe there was something wrong."

Bobby looked at her. "Why?" His eyes narrowed slightly. "Why should anything have been wrong?"

The level intensity of his gaze unnerved her. "I don't know. I just thought...for a minute there you looked...funny."

He turned back to the pink sky. "Was there anything wrong with the way I handled her?"

Charlie heard the challenge in his voice but didn't respond immediately. She was on unsteady ground with this man, and that was something she wasn't used to. Again they seemed to be working on a deeper level than she was prepared for. Instead of talking about Bobby's nervousness on takeoff—which she was still certain had been real, despite his attempts to cover it up—he had managed to turn the conversation into a very intimate one, even though his eyes never left the sky, and his voice barely changed tone. Charlie felt out of her element.

"You handled her very well," she said, watching his handsome profile against the dusky light of early evening.

Now he turned and looked at her, and she felt rather than saw his expression clear again. "What did you expect?" he asked with a lazy grin and a drawl to match.

She grinned back, relieved to find that they were on an easy footing once more. The tension he was able to create in her was confusing. She much preferred this camaraderie. "I expected you to be good."

"I don't know why," he said amiably. "After all, you really don't know anything about me, do you?"

"No, I don't."

"But you knew enough to be sure I'd be good?" His eyes filled with the smoky suggestiveness she found hard to resist. He was right, anyway. She knew almost nothing about him, and yet in a curious way she knew quite a bit. Why couldn't she just relax with Bobby and not waste so much energy trying to figure him out? Why not just trust those famous instincts of hers?

"Let's just say I'm pleasantly surprised," she replied. "I figured you'd be good, but I didn't know you'd be this good!" She looked appreciatively out her window as the plane banked elegantly over a thin wedge of clouds.

He smiled and jauntily raised one eyebrow. "You're full of pleasant surprises, too, you know that, Charlotte Frehling?"

"Charlie," she said, correcting him automatically.

"I know," he said quietly. "Charlie to your friends." The tone of his voice forced her to look at him. "So what should *I* call you, Charlie-to-your-friends?"

She stared at him for a long while, once again thrown into confusion by the light in his eyes. This man kept implicitly demanding things of her; his very presence commanded a very private part of her. She swallowed hard, then decided the only way to deal with his innuendo was not to deal with it. "How about . . . Chief?"

Bobby was silent for a second, and then he threw back his head and laughed, long and loud, breaking the mood so that Charlie was able to laugh with him. "Okay, Chief," he said when he had recovered. "Let's do some real flying."

Bobby flew *Electra* as he would drive a car, with casual expertise, as though the flight course was as familiar as an old country road. Charlie sat back and enjoyed the ride. She was going to like flying with this man, if for no other reason than that he was so good at it.

"You know," she said when they had been silent for a while, "I didn't expect you to be so good with the other Electra."

"You mean the shop? Why, did you think I'd be afraid of a few scraps of linen and silk? I don't scare that easy, you know."

Charlie looked at him quickly, but he didn't seem to have taken offense, in spite of his rather sharp reply. The subject of Bobby's fears, real or not, seemed to make both of them tense.

"No," she replied, steering away from the subject. "Not afraid. Of course not. I just thought it was kind of surprising, the way you got that woman to buy that lynx cape. I mean, I've had four salespeople trying to sell it for nine months, and you just waltzed into the shop, a total stranger to selling, and got her to buy it inside of five minutes."

Bobby winked slyly. "Obviously your people were using the wrong approach."

"So how did you know the right approach? Don't tell me—you used to work in a fancy clothing store before you started flying." Although she knew her theory was absurd, it would have gone a long way toward explaining Bobby's chameleonlike abilities, and the fact that the two of them seemed so well suited to work together. But she knew, even before he laughed and shook his head, that he had never been a salesperson. More likely Bobby's definite charm, which seemed to work on women despite his offhand attitude, was suited to any milieu. Even Marla, she recalled, had blushed when she had come into Charlie's office to announce him.

"You want the real truth?" Bobby asked. "The real truth is that I grew up with four sisters, all of them older than me, and all clotheshorses. You learn a lot about what goes with what in that atmosphere." He glanced down at Charlie's well-fitting jumpsuit. "And what looks good on whom."

Charlie smiled, pleased that he'd noticed. Noticed? His eyes practically raked through the thin material. "Did your sisters wear lynx capes?" she asked, surprised to find her cheeks heating up, even though he was now looking away from her. "They must have been pretty well dressed."

He gave her an odd sideways glance as if unsure whether she was pressing him for more information or simply making conversation. "Let's just say they were pretty resourceful," he said quickly, then fell silent, leaving Charlie to wonder what on earth he meant by *that*. Bobby didn't know it, but his silences raised more questions than any proffered information would have. Then he changed the subject. "But how about you? How did you learn so much about fashion and design?"

"Oh, the regular way. I studied it and worked for other people until I decided what kind of clothes I wanted to make and sell." She told Bobby about her early career, and they laughed together over the tale of her efforts to disabuse people of the notion that she was the lover of her designer-sponsor. "But I guess designing clothes came naturally to me or I wouldn't have pursued it, especially after an experience like that," she added.

"What about flying? Where did you learn so much about that?"

"Flying?" Charlie leaned back in her seat and looked out at the panorama of colors as the sun prepared to set. Bobby was good at getting her to talk about herself. "I suppose I've always wanted to fly, although I didn't know it until I grew up." She turned to him. "You probably knew from the moment you were born, right?"

She expected him to agree and perhaps even to elaborate. But his expression was strange, as though he was looking at something in his past, not at her. When he spoke, however, his voice didn't betray his innermost thoughts, nor did it answer her question. "Do you feel the two things can go together in your life? I mean, your love of flying and your career as a clothing designer?"

"Of course. Why shouldn't they?"

"Then you don't mind mixing business with pleasure on this trip, do you?"

Charlie couldn't tell from his tone if he was asking because he wanted to know more about her, or if he was affirming some private debate. Still, he wasn't asking maliciously, and she felt he deserved an honest answer.

"No, I don't mind business and pleasure together. After all, I enjoy my business as well as the flying. And don't forget that buying up fabric, et cetera, is making it possible for us to pay for this trip."

Perhaps she had spoken the last words more sharply than she had intended, because Bobby was quick to apologize. "Hey, I didn't mean to belittle what you do. I was just curious about what makes you tick." He leaned across the small cockpit, which was rapidly filling with twilit dimness. "I didn't mean to offend you, really." He extended one lean hand. "Friends?"

Charlie looked at his hand for a moment, pale in the growing darkness. She hadn't been offended at all, really, but Bobby seemed always to be one step ahead of her. She had no choice but to accept his apology, even though it was unnecessary. "Friends," she said, smiling and grasping his hand. It was warm and dry, and it held hers easily, fitting as smoothly as a glove. Charlie thought Bobby held on to her hand for a few moments longer than was called for, but she didn't mind in the least. His hand felt nice, and she wouldn't have minded flying along like that for a while, but at that moment he reached up and switched on the cabin lights, then moved the yoke to bank into a turn.

He leaned into the curve easily, luxuriously, obviously feeling the natural arch of the plane all through his body, no doubt right down to the fingers that held the yoke. He was a natural, all right, but that didn't give her a clue to what made him tick. What had brought him to her in the first place? Except for what his résumé and Jim's recommendation had conveyed, she didn't know a thing about Bobby Dupree. She had known he was right for the job, but how had he known the job was right for him? Maybe he was signing on as her copilot simply for the adventure because he had nothing better to do at the moment. Or maybe he was as eager for excitement and glory in the air as she was.

Charlie would just have to assume that, since it felt right to have Bobby aboard, it was. Right now she was having a very good time, and she regretted seeing him head back toward Hancock Field. She hadn't done much night flying; with Bobby it would probably be an adventure worth having.

By the time they had landed and wheeled *Electra* back into her hangar, it was completely dark. Together Charlie and Bobby gave the plane a final checking over. They would probably not get to take her up again before they flew to Hatteras, and they wanted to make sure nothing had gone awry during their short flight. They worked for perhaps an hour, going over the console and the engine bit by bit, murmuring to each other as they systematically checked off each system.

All the time they worked their heads were close together, their faces only inches apart. Charlie and Bobby were so absorbed in *Electra* that neither of them gave any thought to their proximity, or to the fact that Bobby often reached out and touched Charlie lightly when he wanted to show her something, or that Charlie leaned her narrow chin on his shoulder in order to peer into the depths of the engine mount. They were two people totally absorbed by a third presence, the sleek steel bird that would enable them to fulfill their dreams of free flight. The race had captivated both their hearts.

But as soon as they finished the post-flight check, the mood between them changed. As they locked up the plane and walked slowly away from the berth in the cavernous hangar, suddenly they seemed to have very little to say to each other. Each was excruciatingly aware of the other's nearness, and Charlie could almost feel the nubby tweed of the sport coat that Bobby had thrown around his shoulders against the evening chill. He wore no after-shave or lotion; nevertheless, his scent was as clear and tantalizing to her as if he had held a bottle of it under her nose. She caught a glimpse of him silhouetted against the cement floor by the overhead light. Even at that foreshortened angle, he appeared lean and lanky, while the breadth of his shoulders in outline heightened her sense of the real man as they walked together side by side, their eyes trained on the door ahead.

Charlie shivered and drew her thick mohair shawl more closely around her neck. She felt as if there were a conversation buzzing just beyond her hearing, so that she was almost painfully aware of the forced silence between her and Bobby, when only a moment ago there had been intimate talk.

They stopped in the office to check in, then got in Bobby's car. Charlie's M.G. was still at the boutique, and she asked him to drop her off there. If he was disappointed at not being able to take her home, he did a good job of hiding it. They drove in silence through the city, each well aware that the streets were filled with couples on happy outings in Baltimore's newly refurbished harbor area. Charlie wondered if Bobby was thinking the same thing she was—that *their* idea of a good time had been an evening spent dissecting the console panel of a Lear Turbojet. Perhaps they were missing something by not joining the crowds enjoying the warm spring night.

Charlie had just decided that she really *had* preferred poking around *Electra*'s cockpit to wandering through Harbor Place when Bobby pulled up beside her boutique. The shop was closed, but rose-tinted lights in the showroom window revealed mannequins artfully draped in shimmering nylon fabric that stretched up behind them like pennants in a stiff breeze. Charlie was proud of her window displays and gave Bobby a moment to gaze at them with her.

As she turned to see if he had properly appreciated the sight, she found that his face was only inches away from hers, his eyes wide and serious. She gasped at his unexpected closeness, but she didn't pull away.

That was when he kissed her.

It wasn't a long passionate kiss, full of jumbled promises and unexplained impulses. Nor was it a short friendly buss on the cheek. He simply leaned another inch closer and planted his lips warmly but briefly over hers, and she heard his breath rush out in a small sigh of relief as she, surprised, reacted with instinctive pleasure to his touch.

It felt very natural to be kissing Bobby, as long as she didn't give herself a moment to think about what kissing him meant. His mouth was soft and sweet, the undercurrent of hardness in his caress just enough to entice Charlie to press a little harder against him, and to prolong the moment for an instant by settling softly against the back of her seat.

But before she could gather her wits she heard a click. Startled, she pulled away and turned. Bobby, with his free hand, had pushed open the door on the passenger side.

She turned to him, momentarily confused, and he grinned ruefully at her expression. "We've got to keep things on a fairly professional basis, wouldn't you say, Charlie?"

"I . . . uh . . ." Charlie blinked and nodded. At the moment she couldn't verbally answer in the affirmative.

Bobby's voice softened, and it seemed that his drawl became more pronounced. "I mean, I'd be the first one to agree to mixing business with pleasure, especially where you're concerned. . . ." He reached up and traced her lips with his thumb. Involuntarily Charlie closed her eyes. "But we both know what that could lead to. . . ."

Charlie sensed his face moving closer to hers again, but what he was saying made sense. "You're right," she said, her eyes still closed. "Absolutely right."

He drew back. "Right." Charlie opened her eyes to find Bobby smiling genially at her as if nothing out of the ordinary had happened. "So do you want to pick up that flight compass tomorrow, or should I? I want *Electra* flight-ready ASAP, so it should be done first thing in the morning."

"Absolutely. You're right. I'll take care of it first thing." Even as she spoke, smiling back at Bobby and sliding out of the car on her side, Charlie was wondering if she was going crazy. Had he or had he not just kissed her? Now she was standing on the street, and Bobby was watching her, his eyes shadowed by the darkness inside the sedan. He seemed to be waiting for something; she didn't know if the ball was in her court or if he was just being shy.

"Bye!" She waved again, and he waved back but still made no effort to pull away from the curb. "Is something wrong, Bobby?" She peered into the car, almost wishing he would reach out and pull her back in with him to resume that kiss.

"Nope. Nothing wrong. I'm just waiting for you to get into your car. Can't leave you alone out here on the street now, can I?"

So that was it! Chivalry! Charlie almost laughed at her own stupidity. No good Southern boy would have done less . . . and perhaps the kiss sprang from the same gentlemanly impulse.

Perhaps. But she didn't think so. And she hoped not.

TAKEOFF DAY GLEAMED like a jewel full of bright sunshine and promise. Charlie had never been so excited in her life. Everything that had to be done had been done. Even permission for them to vary slightly from the course had come through in the nick of time. The design patterns were all cut, the shopping itinerary planned down to the last detail and the shop left in Marla's competent hands.

And of course *Electra* was in better shape than ever before. Her sleek curvaceous fuselage shone in the clear morning light, and Charlie knew that everything was as perfect inside as it was out. Bobby had seen to that.

Bobby himself looked rakish in his sparkling white overalls, his light brown hair slicked back over his ears. She could see the anticipation glazing his amber eyes, and even his speech was slightly breathless, as if he was saving all his energy for the moment when they would at last take off on the first leg of the journey, from Hatteras to Caracas.

The short flight from Baltimore to Hatteras had been uneventful except for the rowdy early-morning farewell that the Electra sales staff had bestowed on them at the last minute. Charlie had taken the pilot's seat this time, eager to get her hands on *Electra*'s yoke. She wanted to show Bobby how well she handled the little Lear, but Bobby, she noticed, had been fairly tense on takeoff, just as he had been at the controls a few days earlier. This time Charlie put his reaction down to prerace nerves; after all, she was wound up to a fever pitch. Besides, Bobby had his work cut out for him on the short flight. It was his last chance to make sure that *Electra* was in tip-top working order for the long flight to Caracas.

Though there was an optional fuel stop in the Dominican Republic for those jets that didn't have extended flight capacity, *Electra* had been outfitted with extra large wingtip fuel tanks that would make the eighteen-hundred-mile trip possible in one leg. Still, that was a relatively long time for a small jet to be in the air, and both Charlie and Bobby were anxious that the first lap of the trip go off without a hitch. They knew there would be other, more difficult challenges aplenty later on in the race.

The atmosphere at the Cape Hatteras airfield was carnival-like when Bobby and Charlie deplaned to register with the officials. Small business jets dotted the field like colorful sleek nesting birds, while swarms of mechanics clambered around them, doing quick checks and polishing the gleaming exteriors. Well-wishers gathered in knots around their favorites.

Most of the pilots and copilots were in the small terminal awaiting news of their staggered takeoff times as well as any last-minute instructions the race officials might have for them. The air was charged with excitement, but the feeling was warm and friendly, too. Most of the pilots knew each other. Some, like Charlie, were business people who flew their own planes for that purpose and hadn't been able to resist the lure of the race. Others were professional charter pilots hired by businesses. The race was technically open only to small jets in use for business, but several faces were familiar to

Charlie, those of wealthy adventurers who had managed to find a big enough loophole in the race rules to allow them to enter.

In any case, the race had attracted fliers and enthusiasts from around the world—several more, Charlie heard, would be joining them in Caracas—and it was clear that winning the eighth annual circumnavigation of the globe race was bound to be a feather in anyone's cap.

After receiving their flight plan and departure number, Charlie and Bobby left the terminal building to take a brief tour of the field. There were a few old Lears like *Electra*, although none of them sported her snazzy updated features. Most of the planes were much newer than the Lear jet. There were Cessna Citations, Lockheed 1,000s and, most extravagant of them all, the Gulfstream Turbojet III, which rested close to the ground and was slick and shallow in body with wingspans raised at an almost predatory angle.

"Whew," Bobby breathed, standing under the largest model, a silver-bodied beauty with an arched tailwing. "This is some piece of metal."

"About twelve million dollars' worth of metal, to be exact," Charlie said. The Gulfstream was impressive, to be sure, and she knew its capabilities were astounding. But she preferred *Electra*'s more elegant lines and softer style. "*Electra* can do everything that this baby can do," she added defensively.

"Everything? Are you sure of that, Charlotte Frehling?"

The voice came not from Bobby but from somewhere above their heads. Bobby and Charlie looked up and saw someone standing on the rear fuselage of the Gulfstream. The person was dressed in baggy overalls and a painter's cap and was covered almost entirely in grease. But there was something familiar to Charlie about the voice and about the large white teeth that smiled down on her.

It took her a few seconds to place the smile. When she did she let out a whoop of glee. "Karen Michaels, is that you? Come down from that junk heap and say hello!"

"Junk heap—hah! You wish!" Nevertheless, with a loud guffaw Karen made her way inside the plane and out to the wingstep.

"Who's that?" Bobby whispered. He seemed intrigued by the woman's grease-spattered face, and by the idea that this was a woman at all.

"That is Karen Michaels, my old school friend," Charlie said, her voice full of pride and delight. She hadn't seen Karen in over a year, although the two women had been friends ever since grade school, when they had discovered their mutual love of flight.

"Karen Michaels? Not of Michaels Aviation, by any chance, is she? The company that makes flight equipment."

"The same. Alan Michaels is her father. Karen's been working for him for years as a mechanic. She just spent the past year in Japan working on his new factory over there."

"Yep." Karen swung down the short gangplank and gave Charlie a bear hug. "I'm Daddy's chief mechanic— although to this day he can't bear the thought that his darling daughter prefers being a grease monkey to being heiress apparent to Michaels Aviation." She shrugged and extended her hand to Bobby. "Too bad for Pops, but I'm a confirmed greaser."

Bobby looked at the short, stocky woman; in her present state her only identifiable features were a big smile and bright blue eyes. "If what I heard about you is true," he said in his most charming Southern drawl, "then you're doing just what you were meant to do on this earth—and in this sky."

The blue eyes widened slightly. "You mean you've heard of me?" Karen turned to Charlie. "Charlie, where did you find this excellent person? He's heard of me!"

"Karen Michaels, Bobby Dupree. Bobby, Karen." Charlie smiled, but she felt a little bit uncomfortable. Clearly Bobby and Karen shared a certain camaraderie. Karen, it turned out, had heard of Bobby, too. The world of ace jet-plane mechanics was pretty small, and both her friends were full of compliments for each other. Still, Charlie was too delighted to see Karen to worry about the fact that she had much less in common with both of them than they did with each other.

"I should have known you wouldn't miss this race for the world," Karen said, turning to Charlie at last. "But how are you managing to take the time away from the shops?"

"Mixing business with pleasure. I'm doing a lot of buying for my winter line while I'm at it. Sort of mixing the best of both worlds."

Karen greeted this with a good-natured shrug. Although she was a millionaire's daughter, she had never had the least interest in clothes, even as a teenager. Unlike Charlie, her loyalty had been undivided. Flying was all she cared about.

"But what about you?" Charlie asked. "I thought you would still be in Japan. It never occurred to me that you would be back for the race."

"You mean it never occurred to you that Daddy would *let* me come back for the race." Karen grinned ruefully. "It took a lot of doing, believe me. Only his intense desire to have Michaels Aviation equipment show well made him relent. After all, he needed a good copilot, and I am the best." She turned to Bobby and bowed ceremoniously. "Or rather, one of the best."

"I'm willing to share the laurels with you, Ms Michaels," said Bobby, returning her bow with a more chivalrous flourish. "I am in high company, indeed. But I'm curious. . . ." He turned back to the Gulfstream that loomed over their heads. "What are you going to do about the transverse tilt in the engine mount if you hit ocean turbulence? I haven't flown one of these babies in a while, but I hear they've been having a problem with wind shear."

Karen's round face puckered into a smile, and she clicked her tongue happily. "Oh, I'm glad you asked that question—I've been waiting for someone to ask me that question! Step into my parlor, sir, and I'll show you what I've rigged up. I think it's ingenious, if I do say so myself."

Bobby followed Karen to the top of the wing step; then, as an afterthought, turned to Charlie. "Charlie? You coming along?" Karen had already disappeared into the body of the plane.

Charlie waved and shook her head. "No, thanks. I probably wouldn't understand, anyway. I'm going to head back to the terminal and recheck my flight plans with air traffic control. I want to make sure the race officials don't send me off into the Bermuda Triangle."

Bobby returned her wave and disappeared without another word. Charlie walked back to the terminal, trying to talk herself out of feeling left out and unnecessary. Of course Karen and Bobby would have a lot in common! They were both superb mechanics, and the things they talked about would probably sound like

Greek to Charlie, even with her fair-to-middling knowledge of an airplane's inner workings. Bobby as a flyer was another matter. Skilled though he was, Charlie recalled Bobby's tension as he'd taken *Electra* up on his and Charlie's maiden flight together. She recalled a similar strain in his face this morning, even though she'd been at the controls. She had been nervous, of course, but not as tense as Bobby.

Yes, it was important to have a good mechanic, but without a good pilot the plane didn't get off the ground—and she, Charlie Frehling, was as good as they came. Let Bobby and Karen chatter about transverse engine mounts. She had more important things to concern herself with.

By THE TIME *ELECTRA* was set for takeoff early that afternoon, Charlie had forgotten all about her brief bout of insecurity where Bobby was concerned. The hours before takeoff were spent in a flurry of activity, topping up the fuel tanks, checking flight and weather charts and adjusting the computerized controls to the needs of the ocean flight. Charlie had made the trip to Caracas several times, although she had always played copilot to Jim. Now she was too busy to be nervous; besides, having Bobby with her was the best insurance she could imagine against disaster.

During their preflight checkout they had worked side by side, and Charlie felt once again that she had found the perfect foil for her skills in Bobby. What she didn't know about flying he did, and he knew enough about the technical aspect of the trip for them both. She was pleased to see that he had studied the flight charts closely and knew exactly what to expect on the four hour trip.

As it turned out, the flight took almost six. They came up against some strong head winds just north of Haiti and even had to fly slightly east of their flight pattern to avoid a sudden squall that was building high above the coast of the Dominican Republic. But a check with air traffic control told them that all the other planes had had to deal with the same adverse conditions, so they weren't overly concerned about losing precious time.

As a matter of fact, way up there above the blue-green Atlantic, Charlie felt none of the competitive edge that had colored her emotions before takeoff. She knew she was racing against a clock, although the times would be adjusted according to the size and class of each plane. Yet she wasn't anxious in the least. It was so perfectly beautiful—the vault of blue above and below, the endless vista of thick white clouds giving the fliers a patchwork view of the ocean, the sun pouring down over everything with indiscriminate warmth. Charlie just couldn't summon the proper competitive spirit.

Nor was this just another business trip. Oh, she had every intention of dropping in on Electra-Caracas and looking over the inventory, not to mention making a quick check of the local market for some interesting fabrics. But the constraints of her job were gone, just as the constraint of making good time was. Up here at the helm of the trim little Lear jet, her earthbound goals and problems seemed extremely petty, as if seen from the great elevation at which she flew. All that mattered was that she was flying and that she had an entire globe to circle before she need once again commit herself to the pots-and-pans reality of her daily life. For the next few weeks, at least, her world was magic.

And Bobby Dupree would share it all with her. She glanced at him beside her, leaning forward and fiddling intently with the nautical compass he had recently installed. He had seemed stiff beside her for the first few moments of takeoff, and he still wasn't completely at ease, absorbed in his task. But feeling her gaze, he looked over at her and grinned.

"It is perfect, isn't it?"

His words echoed her thoughts exactly. "Couldn't be better," she replied, and they exchanged a long happy look. Bobby and Karen might be kindred spirits as far as their mechanical genius went, Charlie thought, but with her he shared the perfect beauty of flight. Up here at twenty thousand feet they understood each other completely. What happened on the ground—that sudden awkwardness, that chasm of silence—was of no importance whatsoever.

It wasn't until after sunset that they came within radio distance of the tower at Caracas and got their landing clearance. But the sunset, reflected behind them in a frenzy of pink and purple off the curve of the Atlantic, was so lovely that both were loathe to descend into their landing pattern.

"Someday," said Bobby, staring out the window, "once I get myself up here I'm not going to want to come down. I'm just going to want to stay up here forever and ever."

Charlie realized that Bobby was revealing something very private about himself with this unexpected admission. "Why?" she asked softly, unwilling to break the mood. "Why would you want to stay up here forever?"

He turned slowly to look at her, his face half in shadow and backlit so that his hair glowed like molten gold. His eyes, too, seemed to glow from within as he watched her. "Because I have everything I want up here," he said gently. "Why should I bother going down?"

Charlie thought she understood what he meant, yet there was a negative undercurrent to the words. She was stunned when he suddenly placed one long hand against her neck, flicking aside her hair and tenderly stroking there. It was a brief gesture, just as their one kiss had been brief. But it was far from meaningless. His touch on the sensitive skin at her nape sent heat down her spine, so that Charlie had to grip the yoke more tightly for a moment to keep from trembling. She wanted to feel his touch forever, yet she knew she wouldn't be able to concentrate on her descent if he didn't move his hand right away.

He did. With one last flick of a fingertip it was gone, and Bobby was once again the perfect copilot. "Pull up there," he said, pointing with his chin to a slight tilt to the port side. "There's a fairly strong current on the left."

Charlie obeyed and brought the plane down for a perfect landing. Normally, as much as she enjoyed flying, she felt no real regard about coming down to earth. The euphoria she found in the sky, which made everything on the ground seem of little importance, quickly disappeared as her enthusiasm for the other aspects of her life grew. After all, terra firma was where her successful business was, and she enjoyed the Electra boutiques as much as she enjoyed the *Electra* of the skies. Well, almost as much.

But this time, there was no contest. Like Bobby—with Bobby—Charlie felt she could have stayed in the limitless world of blue forever.

TAKEOFF AND LANDINGS, Charlie soon realized, were destined to be rituals combining the usual customs and airport rigmarole of each country with the FAI's protracted check-in procedure. By the time she and Bobby got to their hotel in Caracas, it was quite late, after 9:00 P.M. Fortunately, however, the South American dinner hour had barely started, and so after hastily showering and changing in their rooms, Charlie and Bobby met in the flowered lobby of the elegant Royal Caracas Hotel. All race contestants had been invited to a first-stop dinner in the grand courtyard of the hotel. Charlie, having spent all day in a casual teal blue jumpsuit, had eagerly chosen one of her favorite designs for the occasion—a creamy silk tunic with wide shoulders and a deep-yoked V trimmed with the softest butter-colored pigskin. The huge batwing sleeves were similarly lined, and there was a matching leather tie slung low around her hips. The effect was tailored yet elegant, and Bobby's admiring double take when she descended the palm-lined staircase was gratifying.

"One of yours?" he asked, taking her arm and linking it through his as if this was the most natural gesture in the world.

"One of mine." Again Charlie was struck by the difference between their airborne and landlocked relationships. If Bobby had taken her arm while on board *Electra*, she would have thought nothing of it. Here, though, it sent unexpected and uneasy shivers of pleasure up her arm and into her chest.

"It's stupendous," he said warmly, although he seemed to be paying more attention to her luminous lavender eyes, edged tonight with a simple line of violet kohl to bring out their color.

"Thank you," she replied, demurely ducking her head, but her smile was hardly demure. "You're looking awfully nice yourself this evening, Mr. Dupree."

He was, too. Somehow, somewhere, Bobby had come up with the perfect tropical suit. Of bone-white linen and double-breasted, it fit his lean frame with an elegance that suggested a life of moneyed privilege, hardly that of an aeronautics mechanic. On Bobby, who always looked as if he'd been born in casual attire, the effect was startling, both because of the natural way he moved in the suit and because of the contrast to his everyday attire.

He shrugged off the compliment with a lopsided grin. "Oh, this is just a little something I dug up somewhere. Shall we go in to dinner, Ms Frehling?"

Charlie knew enough about good fabric and cut to know the suit was hardly "a little something." It was expensive and tailored to his body. The only thing she couldn't figure out was how he had managed to pull it, perfectly pressed, from the army-green duffel bag that was his only luggage. Charlie herself, having made a tremendous effort to travel light, had brought along two suitcases and an overnight bag for the three-week trip.

She had no desire to press the issue. It was enough to be entering the banquet area—a huge open atrium in the middle of the hotel, lined with fragrant blossoms and strung with lights—on the arm of such an arresting companion. Charlie looked forward with mischievous pleasure to the stares she knew she and Bobby would receive when they told people they were pilot and copilot—and who was who.

They had been placed at a table set back among huge pots of flowering jasmine—the scent was almost overpowering. Charlie was glad to see that Karen and her pilot were at the same table. Karen looked even more unusual out of work clothes than Bobby did, but her simple blue shirtwaist brought out the gay sparkle in her eyes, and Charlie noted with approval that her old friend had used some makeup and had styled her hair. She looked happy and excited.

The same couldn't be said for Karen's pilot, whom she introduced as Devon Ross, a name that was unfamiliar to Charlie but obviously struck an unwelcome bell for Bobby; he offered his hand to the man with uncustomary curtness. Despite the warm evening air, Devon was wearing a white shirt and leather bomber jacket, and he sprawled in his seat with the bored manner of a man making an appearance among his inferiors purely for form's sake.

"So, Dupree, you've signed on for that little Lear, have you?" His British accent didn't quite ring true to Charlie's ears. "That ought to be about your speed, I suppose."

"*Electra*'s not a Gulfstream," Bobby retorted, "but she'll do just fine, Devon, believe me. And yes, she's exactly my speed." There was an odd challenge in Bobby's golden eyes that made them look faintly menacing, like a large cat's. "You can do a lot of flying in these old babies, you know. It's not like flying by computer, but it's a lot more . . . real."

Devon smiled faintly and turned away, unwilling to dignify this remark with an answer. Karen, slightly red, stepped into the silence. "Well," she said heartily, "our jet is not exactly a computer, you know—but I understand what you mean about *Electra*. I took her up once when Charlie had just gotten her, and she is a little dreamboat."

"I need a drink," Devon said, and left the table with a perfunctory nod. Bobby stared after him with narrowed eyes.

"Do you know him well?" Charlie inquired. The two men had obviously met before, and it was equally obvious that neither wished to renew the acquaintance.

"I've run into him before," was all Bobby would say.

"My father hired Devon about six years ago as his test pilot and personal air chauffeur," Karen said with an apologetic smile. "He's . . . he can be a little rough sometimes, but he's one of the best in the business." Her half laugh was self-deprecating. "Dad wouldn't let me take the Gulfstream out for this race unless I agreed to let Devon pilot her. I think it was as much trouble for Devon to accept me as it was for me to accept him." Then her good nature reasserted itself. "But he is terrific at the controls, and really, that's what counts in a race like this—good teamwork."

"You bet." Bobby, too, had regained his composure, and now he slapped Charlie lightly on the back. "And that's what we've got here, too. Frehling and Dupree, out to conquer the world!"

The slap on the back surprised Charlie a bit, but she appreciated Bobby's enthusiasm. His high spirits were infectious; soon everybody at the table was regaling each other with tales of past triumphs and plans for future glories. The circumnavigation race, in its eight-year history, had already established quite a reputation among serious fliers as well as among entrepreneurs who flew their own jets. The race seemed to attract a group of highly motivated men and, to a lesser extent, women who lived their successful lives by their own rules. It appealed to the adventurer in the businessman and, since the prestige of winning often led to lucrative job offers, to the businessman in the professional flier. The combination of business and pleasure lured many people besides Charlie.

But this was her first such race, and her excitement was mixed with dizzying anticipation of the unknown. She had flown to Caracas before and had even stopped off once or twice on the West African coast en route to Elec-

tra-Nice. But she had never ventured farther on her own,
to the unexplored lands to the east with their exotic
names and reputations. The prospect of seeing those new
worlds excited her as much as the challenge of flying
there herself. Her designer's eye and her aviator's in-
stinct told her the experience she was about to under-
take would change her life forever.

The evening was a huge success, fostering the spirit of
camaraderie as well as a healthy competitiveness among
the contestants, who hailed from around the globe.
Charlie circulated after dinner, greeting old acquaintances and making new ones. The consensus was that
Charlie was taking on a considerable challenge, circum-
navigating the globe in *Electra*. Some in attendance implied that her budget and experience were fairly limited
for such an endeavor. But this generally was not a crowd
that passed judgment; she got more encouragement than
disapproval from her peers.

The only sour note in the evening was finding Bobby
and Karen, their chairs pulled together so that they sat
knee to knee, deep in a discussion of wing flaps and rudders. It wasn't that Charlie was jealous of Karen—she
knew her old friend too well for that. But she still felt left
out of their tightly knit circle of mutual respect and
wished she could contribute to their discussion with the
same knowledge and fervor. Somehow, knowing as
much as she did about fashion struck her as a superficial
talent to possess in this situation. Surely it took greater
skill to design a plane.

This insecurity was unfamiliar to Charlie, and it was
coupled with another less worthy feeling. If Bobby could
sit so easily with Karen, his blondish head next to hers,
his knees touching hers in thoughtless intimacy, what did
this say about the intimacy he'd shared with Charlie?

There was really no magic between them, after all—he and Karen would be as perfect a team as he and Charlie. It was Bobby himself who created the magic because of his intense love of flying. He would create it anywhere, with anyone.

On the whole, though, the evening was a success. By the time her head hit the pillow after 1:00 A.M., Charlie was too exhausted to give the matter of Bobby Dupree more than a moment's thought; she fell into a deep and dreamless sleep. She had made plans to meet him very early the following morning. She wanted to visit Electra-Caracas before they took off, and Bobby said he wanted to make a quick trip to the airfield to make sure *Electra* had spent a good night, since, as he said, "she wasn't used to camping outside."

But his knock on her door at 6:00 A.M. fell on deaf ears. Charlie was so exhausted that she didn't even hear the jangle of her travel alarm. She might even have slept through her seven o'clock wake-up call if a hand on her shoulder hadn't jarred her into instant alertness.

"Who . . . ? What . . . ?" She sat bolt upright in bed, momentarily disoriented and unable to recognize the intruder.

"Relax. It's only me," said Bobby, and he sat still on the bed next to her, his hand gently massaging her shoulder until he saw that she knew him for a friend.

"How did you get in here?" Charlie was perplexed but remembered to run a hand through her long tangle of hair, pushing the silky strands out of her face and at the same time surreptitiously sweeping the sleep from her eyes.

"By the balcony, of course," he said with a grin, indicating the open sliding doors that led onto a bougainvillea-strewn porch on the hotel's third floor. "I climbed down from my room on the fourth—" he chuckled "—and nearly scared some old man to death when I landed on his porch instead of yours."

Charlie smiled sleepily at the image of Bobby bowing politely to a startled old gent in striped pajamas. "But why didn't you use the door? Most people do, even here in Venezuela."

"I did. I knocked my knuckles raw, to no avail. Do you always sleep that deeply?"

"Deeply? Why? What time is it?" She turned to her alarm clock and gasped, "6:10? You're kidding! You mean I really didn't hear you? Or my alarm?" She was genuinely shocked, since under normal circumstances she was a light sleeper and an early riser. "Oh, God, I'm sorry, Bobby. I'm not usually so lazy. I—"

"Hey." The hand that still lay on her shoulder gave it a gentle squeeze. "You have every reason to be exhausted. And, anyway, I kind of enjoyed the early-morning balcony scene. It got my blood running."

Charlie looked at him and shook her head. "You're crazy, you know that? Jumping balconies at 6:00 A.M...."

Bobby shrugged. "Any Romeo worth his salt would have done the same," he pointed out. With an appreciative look downward, he smiled. "Although I doubt many Juliets have provided such a pleasing countenance on waking as you do."

Charlie looked down and was reminded that she was wearing next to nothing. One of her private penchants was to wear exquisite, if slightly exotic, lingerie wherever she was. For a woman who prided herself on the absolute practicality of the clothes she designed, Charlie's nightwear was an incongruous frivolity. Almost half of one suitcase was full of frothy lace—silk nighties, slips and underwear in various shades from bridal white to deep red.

Last night she had put on a pale aquamarine gown with ecru lace at the bodice—what there was of the bodice. Actually it was really two thin strips of sheerness that began just under her breasts and spread over them and up to cross her shoulders and join at her nape. What there was of the lace was sheer enough, but the deep V between her breasts, which were accented and separated by the lace, revealed a greater expanse of creamy skin than most women would consider decent, even for sleepwear.

Instinctively her hands went to cover her nakedness, but Bobby just laughed and reached out to pull them away. "Don't be silly," he said lightly. "I'm the one with four sisters, remember? And, anyway, as lovely as they are, your charms are the last thing I should have on my mind at this moment. After all, you're the boss around here, and we do have a pretty full day ahead of us, and we're late as it is. . . ."

Despite the practicality of his chatter, something very strange was happening as Bobby spoke to her. His face seemed to be moving closer and closer, and his hands, which had gently grasped her wrists to pull them away from her breasts, were moving back to that spot. Even stranger, thought Charlie as Bobby's words ran down into silence, was that she, without any conscious intention, seemed to be moving closer to *him*. She was definitely aware of her body tilting forward, so that the thin cotton sheet fell away to her waist, revealing even more silk and lace.

And it was her hands that pulled Bobby's hands back to cover her breasts. She waited until they lay firmly across each orb of flesh before lifting her arms to encircle his neck and pull him closer yet. The room was suddenly filled with a heavy silence, so that both of them heard the melody of a faraway songbird with unnatural clarity.

"I don't . . . I'm not sure . . ." Charlie began to speak, trying to give voice to the rational side of her that should surely be protesting this unexpected turn of events.

Bobby stilled her. "Lady," he murmured, "you better hush. This is bigger than both of us right now." And then his lips were on hers, and there was no more time for speech, much less rational thought.

Locked together in an embrace of mutual discovery, they slipped back down amid the crisp sheets of the double bed. The bougainvillea must have just opened, Charlie thought, because the room was filled with the most remarkably heady fragrance as if a thousand blossoms had just been crushed beneath them as they lay down. The ripe floral scent was mixed with the muskier odor of Bobby, who pressed himself against her in her silky gown, as though by sheer willpower he could eradicate the clothing separating their flesh.

"God," he muttered, his voice ragged against her ear, "I've waited so long to do this to you...to touch you...."

"Bobby. . ." Charlie began, not knowing how she was going to finish the sentence, and then realized she had nothing to say. His lips, it seemed, never stopped moving, exploring the contours of her mouth, nose and chin, moving up to her eyelids and down her throat. The only sound she could make then was a low, lingering sigh, a quaver of abandonment that Bobby silenced by pressing his lips even more avidly to hers.

One of his hands tangled in the wealth of her hair, raking through it as though he expected to find gold among the strands. His other hand stretched down the length of her thigh, caressing the silk and inflaming the sensitive skin beneath.

It was his hands, finally, that convinced Charlie she wanted to make love to Bobby more than anything in the world. His hands—so long and lean and elegant, so strong and capable. Her entire body seemed to purr beneath his expert ministrations, tuned to a fine pitch of sensitivity unlike anything she had known before. To have resisted such perfect pleasure would have been impossible.

Her hands moved up to stroke his long blondish mane and to frame his hard, lean jaw. His face was taut with desire and with the effort to control it, but his eyes were soft and half-closed. When he felt her looking at him, he opened them more fully and smiled. His smile, and hers in response, constituted a perfect dialogue. They both recognized their intense need to love and be loved by each other, their intense physical attraction underscored by some as yet unnamed emotional connection that neither of them had really expected to find. Closing their eyes, they abandoned themselves once more to their bodies. Charlie slipped her hands around Bobby's neck and, tightly locking her fingers, held him as if afraid he might pull a millimeter away and sever the magnetic link. Even when he lifted her body off the bed and slipped her nightgown down around her waist, then over her hips, leaving her nude and expectant beneath him on the sheets, she didn't dare release her hold.

"Wait," he whispered, lifting his arms and trying to pry her fingers apart so that he could remove his own clothing. "I promise I won't go away."

Reluctantly she let go, and he kneeled above her on the bed to slip his shirt over his head, his eyes scarcely leaving the creamy expanse of Charlie's hips and thighs or the swiftly tightening areolas of her nipples as she waited impatiently for his body to cover hers. His gaze was as arousing as his touch had been, and now, as he stood to remove his pants, she saw that he, too, had reached a fever pitch of desire that could no longer be held at bay.

For a moment he was still, standing above her, his lean musculature suffused with light from the rising sun streaking through the room from the open curtains behind him. Then he lay over her again, and she felt the torrid heat from his flesh against her own. His hands were torches of heat as they raked over her breasts and loins. She stroked his body hungrily, stoking the already white-hot fire of his need for her. His fingers explored the intimate recesses of her body, taking perfect inventory of her pulses and desires and gauging her heat. But he was also an artist, and the kisses he rained over her body were as tender as his hands were clever.

Charlie was ready, all too soon, to have him enter her. Her body arched against his. But Bobby held off, poised over her, all lean rippling muscle and hardness, his mouth devouring her flesh until her nipples ached and her thighs burned to receive him.

"This is a moment to last forever," he said, guessing at her impatience from the needy arch of her torso toward his. "I mean to make it last as long as that—at least as long as that."

But the hunger in his voice, which rendered his drawl thicker and bittersweet, was more than she could bear, and Charlie shook her head wildly from side to side. "No, please," she whispered. "We don't have forever . . . we only have now. Now!"

If her eyes had been open, she would have seen the flash of light in Bobby's eyes. But they were not, and the moment passed quickly as, with a deep growl of urgency, Bobby moved over and into her. Then there was no more delicate sunlight and mysterious floral fragrance, but the deeper primal scent and color of passion. Charlie responded to Bobby's exultant thrusts and lingering revolutions with a primitive immediacy she wouldn't have believed possible for her. The gay tropical atmosphere of the Caracas hotel room had changed into the heated steaminess of a jungle, and she was a jungle creature, clinging and loving with every pore of her being.

It was a long time before the heat of the moment evaporated into the normal air of the Venezuelan morning, and longer still before Bobby and Charlie, locked in a damp and seamless embrace, realized that the ringing in their ears was from the telephone beside the bed.

Satiated and lazy, Bobby groped clumsily to pick it up. Without speaking into the receiver, he handed the phone across his chest to Charlie, who lay groggily on top of him, her tangled hair spread like a liana across his loins. She had to clear her throat several times before the words would come out comprehensibly. "Hello . . . ?"

The voice on the other end was obviously used to such grogginess. "Señorita Frehling?" it said with crisp cheerfulness. "This is your wake-up call. It's seven o'clock."

"Seven o'clock? Wake-up call?" She was still having trouble orienting herself.

"That's right, *señorita*," said the voice. "Have a nice day!"

5

HAVE A NICE DAY, indeed!

Charlie couldn't believe what had just happened to her. Not that she regretted it—it had been too magical and too satisfying for regrets. Still, it seemed impossible to her that, after hanging up the old-fashioned black receiver on its Buddha-like base, she should turn and see Bobby, lying naked and very much at ease...on her bed.

She tried to make her grin playful and insouciant. "Well, well, well. *That* wake-up call I didn't miss."

"You might have slept through that one, too, if not for me." Bobby seemed totally at ease. He lay among the sheets as casually as if he were lounging beside her in the cockpit of *Electra*. "I think," he added with a wicked tilt to his eyebrow, "that you owe me a debt of thanks."

He leaned toward her, ready to collect his debt, but Charlie moved back. "Listen, Bobby."

He drew back slightly himself, but didn't look offended. "Yes?" he drawled.

Faced with his clear amber eyes and serene half smile, Charlie grew flustered. Didn't he feel awkward in the least? Obviously not. Biting her lip, she tried to keep her eyes from roaming the length of his body.

"I think ... well ... perhaps it would be ..." He was giving her no help at all, and Charlie's voice trailed off. "What should we do about this?" she asked plaintively.

"About this?" Bobby's expansive gesture took in both their bodies, the rumpled bed and the light-filled room. Charlie snuck a look—he was marvelous looking, that was for sure. "What's there to do? Except maybe do it again, of course." Again that mischievous glint came into his eyes, and again Charlie pulled back as he leaned forward.

"Bobby, no. I mean, don't you think . . ."

This time he leaned back with a sigh. "Don't I think this was a big mistake? That we should never have risked our professional relationship by hitting the sack?" Despite his gentle drawl, the words sounded brutal, and Charlie winced. Yes, that was exactly what she had been thinking, but she hadn't expected the words to sound so . . . cold.

"Well?" he demanded. "Is that what you think I should think?" The amber eyes flashed hot gold for a moment, causing Charlie to lower hers.

"Something like that," she muttered.

When he spoke again his voice was gentle. "Actually," he told her with a soft smile, "I hadn't been thinking anything of the sort. But I can understand your position, Charlie." He reached for her hand, and Charlie didn't pull it away. "Look, what just happened between us was inevitable. We could no more have stopped it than we could have stopped that sunrise. Do you believe that?"

She met his earnest gaze and nodded. "I do. Of course I do." The memory of their lovemaking was too fresh in her mind—and in her body—for her to deny its power.

"Then the only thing we can do is accept it, and get on with our lives." He gave her hand a little squeeze of reassurance. "Believe me, Charlie, it'll be easier than you think."

How did he know? Charlie wondered. Had he done this so many times before? Bobby must have read the question in her expression, because he laughed. "I don't know why I know that, so don't start pegging me as some sex-crazed gigolo." His voice softened. "But I know we can't erase what happened, and I for one would never want to try. If you like," Bobby went on, "I'll just shinny up the balcony and we can pretend the whole thing was just a dream—a delicious, fabulously real dream." The hand that still held hers caressed it for a moment. "Is that what you'd like? You can close your eyes, and I'll dress and slip out of here and come around to knock at your door as if I were just coming to wake you up."

The idea was so genuinely thoughtful—and so elaborately ludicrous—that Charlie burst out laughing. "I don't think we have to go quite that far, Bobby. Exiting by the door will do just fine."

He was already on the edge of the bed pulling on his jeans. "You're the pilot," he said, and looked over his shoulder at her with a grin. "You say bail out the door, I bail out the door."

He slipped his sneakers on and, carrying his T-shirt over one arm, bent down to the bed to give her one last kiss. "Sorry about this," he said as his lips connected with hers, "I promise it'll never happen again."

Before she could protest, or even decide if she wanted to protest—he was up and at the door. He had his hand on the latch when she called his name.

"Bobby?"

He turned, and part of her ached to call him back to her bed. He looked so lovely there, straight and bare-backed, his golden hair gleaming in the full morning sun.

"Yes?" he said hopefully.

Charlie stared at him for a moment, then smiled and shook her head. "I just want you to know," she said at last, "that I won't forget, either. I couldn't even if I tried."

Bobby winked. "Ma'am," he said as he opened the door, "I know exactly what you mean."

STILL, IT WAS HARDER to focus on the day's flight than Charlie would have expected. She got up as soon as Bobby left, called room service for coffee and sweet bread and washed and packed while she waited for her breakfast tray. She was in no mood to go down to the dining room and mingle with the other fliers. It was taking all her considerable energies to put her brain in proper working condition.

So while she sat out at the little wrought-iron table on her balcony and sipped the hot coffee with steaming sweetened milk, she allowed herself several moments to luxuriate in the questions and conundrums she knew would rise to haunt her later if she didn't give them due time now. How, for instance, had a simple, friendly wake-up visit turned into a careening passionate interlude? Hadn't there been any warning, or had Charlie been blind to all the signs that usually heralded a romantic attraction. Yes, there had been moments of awkwardness with Bobby, interspersed with moments of complete ease—that might have been a clue. But she had put her reactions down to other things, certainly not to an intimate attraction. She wasn't so sure about Bobby's feelings. Perhaps he had planned something like this all along, or had simply found her in a vulnerable moment and made the very best of it.

She couldn't deny that the experience had been powerful, nor that if she hadn't wanted intimacy, he wouldn't have made the slightest move in her direction. She assumed equal responsibility for the lovemaking, but that didn't answer the question of why, or how, or even more important, what next?

Nevertheless, she refused to allow their romantic interlude to interfere with their flying. If it meant going as far as ignoring the chemistry between them, well, she was willing to pay that price. If Bobby alluded to their morning tryst, she would have to tell him quite firmly that she had no intention of bringing up the subject again, and that she would appreciate the same from him.

But Bobby was perceptive. He read her like a book, and she was confident that if she didn't want him to refer to the incident, he wouldn't. It was herself she distrusted. Would she really be able to conduct business as usual? To spend hours alone with Bobby Dupree in that little cockpit without thinking about the power of his arms, his strong thighs, his lips? Would she be able to talk to him about altitudes, latitudes and longitudes without recalling the husky sounds he had uttered in the midst of their passion, or watch him fiddle with a control without imagining his touch on her breasts?

There was no question about it—she simply *had* to. She had a plane to fly, a business to run and a race to win, and she trusted that her competitive spirit and her will to succeed would give her the strength she couldn't summon now, sitting only a few feet away from where they had been together.

Charlie finished her breakfast and dressed with an air of resolution. She put on a steel-gray cotton jumpsuit with short capped sleeves and a simple elastic waist—no need to dress up when she would be spending over ten hours in the air today. She drew her hair up into its customary knot on her head and dabbed on her makeup with determined nonchalance. Her only concessions to the momentous morning were a pair of suede high heels and a slash of fuchsia lipstick. After all, she was going to Electra-Caracas, and one didn't appear on Caracas's most fashionable shopping street without attempting to look suitably chic.

After arranging to have her luggage shipped out to the airfield, Charlie took a taxi to her boutique. Electra-Caracas had been the third of the Electra shops to open, and to Charlie it still represented the most daring outpost in her little fashion empire. After all, Baltimore and New York were all-American cities, and American women had long been clear about what they wanted to buy. Even Electra-Nice, with its Mediterranean flair, was a logical outpost for the fresh sporty look for which Charlie Frehling was known.

But Caracas? Charlie had never suspected that she would end up with a shop here, nor that the women of the Venezuelan capital would welcome her with such open arms. She had come on a buying trip through South America several years earlier and had been struck at once by the distinctive style of the women who paraded up and down Caracas's main thoroughfares. Tall and elegant, they moved with a special ease in their couture clothes. Immediately, Charlie had envisioned them in her own designs, realizing that her loosely tailored fit would perfectly suit the tropical climate. Her business manager had found her a vacant shop, but only with great reluctance had he been persuaded to let her invest in a long-term lease.

Electra-Caracas had been a hit from the start. The *caraqueñas* had flocked to her door, buying quantities of Charlie's low-waisted floral print dresses in nearly sheer chiffon, or her pale-toned one-piece pantsuits that slid coolly over the body, revealing sensuous body lines and allowing unfettered movement of the arms and legs. She often designed patterns especially for this market, although she had learned that whatever sold well in Caracas was sure to sell well in her other three stores.

This morning Charlie's entire sales staff had gathered to greet her, not because she came so rarely—she usually made the trip at least three or four times a year—but because they, too, wanted to give a warm send-off to their airborne namesake. They sat through their customary sales meeting with big smiles and giggled and whispered while Charlie made her usual stocktaking tour of the merchandise, both in Electra and in a few other carefully chosen boutiques. Her summer line was still selling well and would do so, she presumed, well into December; the Venezuelan summer was now in full swing.

The staff waited until Charlie was about to get into a taxi for the airport before they produced streamers, glitter and champagne. They tossed streamers and glitter at Charlie as they would at a bride, covering her steel-gray suit and her hair with fairy dust and bits of bright color. She was instructed to break the champagne over *Electra*'s bow or, in the absence of a suitable moment for such a dedication, imbibe it with the good wishes of the Caracas-Electra staff in mind.

Charlie then sped off toward the airfield, buoyed by the stability of the shop as well as the goodwill of her staff. Even the prospect of seeing Bobby again didn't daunt her. She checked in with air traffic control, customs and the race officials, who asked an inordinate number of questions about her hour-long disappearance from their sphere of authority. Charlie assured them that she had gotten clearance from the American branch of the FAI to conduct her own business in various ports of call, should they suppose she had been meeting with saboteurs who had only the destruction of the FAI and the race in mind.

Business behind her, Charlie walked out to *Electra*, her mind already gearing up for the ordeal ahead. It was still early, but she knew the day's flight would be a long one—from Caracas to Recife, Brazil, for refueling, and then on to Dakar—a total distance of over three thousand miles—about twice what they had done the day before. They wouldn't land at Dakar until late that night, and Charlie knew she would need her wits about her, particularly during those last long hours when they would have to rely on instruments rather than sight.

But she was eager to take off, and when she saw Bobby, she knew at once that he, too, had only one thing on his mind—the race. "I checked the weather reports all the way through," he told her by way of greeting when she reached the plane. "It looks like we should have smooth sailing and a nice tail wind, especially after we leave Recife and get out over the South Atlantic."

"Yes, I heard." Charlie fell gratefully into the business at hand. "I remember that the South Atlantic was an easy crossing. Good jet streams and not much turbulence if you hit the right day."

The radio crackled from the tower, giving *Electra* clearance to taxi into takeoff position. "Well," said Bobby, sliding smoothly into the copilot seat and adjusting his earphones, "it looks to me like this is going to be one of those days."

BOBBY WAS RIGHT. The flight was gorgeous, even more spectacular than that of the day before. From Caracas to Recife they hugged the coast, gazing down on verdant foliage and an aquamarine sea. It was almost six hours before they reached Recife for refueling, but the time seemed to fly by as quickly as the fluffy white clouds that occasionally scudded below them.

They landed in Recife and took off again almost immediately, with time only for a pit stop and check-in with the ever-present race officials. Recife was a sleepy airport in the midday heat, and the locals were clearly unaccustomed to hordes of fliers congesting their narrow runways in the middle of what should have been siesta.

The takeoff from Recife was a little rocky. A sudden head wind made *Electra* stumble on her ascent, and Charlie had to do some quick maneuvering to regain stability. Her eyes were glued to the windshield and her control panel, her hands wedded to the yoke that guided the plane up past the cloud line. She occasionally spoke to Bobby without looking at him, giving instructions that she could tell had already been carried out before they were issued.

It wasn't until they reached five thousand feet and *Electra* was humming along nicely that she turned to Bobby, a smile of triumph on her face.

"A little bit of fancy flying to wake us up, huh?" She was proud of the way she had handled the minor crisis. It had also made her realize that flying around the world was probably not going to be as uncomplicated as it had been so far. Flying a small jet wasn't just a matter of takeoffs and landings and reading instrument panels, and Charlie was glad of that. This excitement was part of what she loved most about flying her own plane, the feeling of being in charge, of controlling her fate.

Bobby obviously didn't feel the same way. When she looked at him, he was sitting rigidly in his seat, and his complexion was decidedly pale. This was the third time

Charlie had noticed his nervousness, and she decided now was the time to bring it out into the open.

"Bobby, what on earth is wrong with you?"

Bobby turned his head stiffly and managed a weak smile. "Wrong? Nothing's wrong."

"Don't tell me nothing's wrong. Every time we take off you get green around the gills. Are you all right?"

"Yes, of course I'm all right." He was fast looking better. "It's just . . . you know, preflight jitters. Everybody gets them. Or rather most people get them." Now fully recovered, he reached out and patted her on the shoulder. "Some of us, on the other hand, are such aces that it never even occurs to us to be frightened. You're an ace, Charlie, a real ace."

Charlie didn't reply. She had only experienced preflight jitters occasionally and for a good reason, like the first time she had flown solo, or the day she'd gone up for her instrument rating. But she knew many fliers got nervous on takeoff or landing as a matter of routine, and she had certainly never held that against them.

Why did she feel Bobby should be exempt? Despite natural ability, there was no such thing as a perfect flier. Every pilot had his or her weak spot and was taught to identify it during flight training. A pilot also learned to compensate for it with either a copilot who balanced out the weakness or with a safety net in terms of extra instrumentation. Some pilots tended to get disoriented during twilight flying; some had difficulty correctly gauging air distances. And some got nervous on takeoff.

Bobby should be different, though. Not perfect, but fearless, and certainly in command of his emotions. After all, his behaviour that morning had revealed a man very much in control of a situation. Of course that had been a different circumstance—very, very different, and Charlie had promised herself not to think about it. Even the briefest recollection threatened to unsettle her equilibrium. She wasn't about to lose her cool eighteen thousand feet above the South Atlantic. Besides, by now Charlie understood Bobby well enough to know that if he wasn't offering any further explanation for his behaviour, she wasn't going to get one from him by insisting.

In fact, all other considerations were superseded by the endless minutiae that flying a small plane over a large body of water engendered. During the next six hours there was scarcely a moment when one or the other wasn't directly involved in some aspect of the flight—one simply didn't point the tiny Lear in the right direction and wait to sight land. The constant changes in light, wind and speed had to be accounted for, and radio contact had to be maintained to ensure that the ever-changing South Atlantic didn't spring an unexpected storm on them.

The race commission had provided every team with a box supper, but as darkness swiftly covered the silvery sea below and enveloped them in blackness, they found they had no time even to eat. They required every ounce of their energy to ride steady in the unaccustomed darkness, where not even an occasional ship's light lent the comfort of orientation.

By the time they sighted land on the westernmost tip of Senegal in Africa, it was 10:00 P.M. They received radio instruction that they would have to circle for a while, since there had been a delay in the landing order of the flights preceding theirs. There was some comfort in the sight of city lights below them, but Bobby and Charlie were both too exhausted to feel any of the exhilaration that normally accompanies a first trip to an exotic place.

They couldn't even muster much pleasure over the fact that they had clocked in a very creditable average of 196 miles per hour on the second leg of the journey. This was a good speed for any small business jet in their weight class, and excellent for a plane like *Electra*.

All either of them could think about was a warm shower and a soft bed—alone. Sleep seemed like the most sensual luxury in the world to Charlie; she yearned to slip between the sheets. When they finally got clearance to land, it was all she could do to bring *Electra* in smoothly on the rough tarmac of the Dakar runway.

It was well past midnight by the time they landed, went through the customs and debriefing rituals, left instructions with the ground crew for *Electra* and found a taxi to take them to their hotel. As they sped by, Charlie tried to look out the window and soak in the teeming nightlife of the strange city, but her vision blurred as a result of fatigue and eyestrain. All she could see was a smudge of color and a dim outline of low white buildings along the interminably winding streets.

IT WASN'T UNTIL she woke up the next day that the pleasure of her situation hit her. The FAI officials had arranged for a thirty-six hour layover in Dakar and, after having slept for eleven hours undisturbed on the narrow but comfortable bed, she felt both relaxed and energized. She planned to do a lot of shopping in the capital city and had a long list of large and small fabric warehouses to visit. After the excitement and strain of the past three days, she was ready to forget about *Electra* the plane for a while and concentrate on Electra the boutique.

The hotel Charlie and Bobby were staying in was small and old, but elegant in its quiet way. Charlie dressed in

a cool white tent dress. She was tired of wearing jumpsuits, and besides, the sun outside her wooden louvered
window was already very hot. She was a little disappointed but not at all surprised to find that Bobby wasn't
in the dining room. Another pilot told her he'd been and
gone over an hour ago. Probably out to the airport to
check on *Electra*, she thought, and sat down to her thick
steaming coffee and sweet rolls, satisfied that everything was being taken care of.

After breakfast she called Karen's room on the extremely unlikely chance that her friend might be interested in accompanying her to the shops, mills and
bazaars. Karen wasn't in, and in the end Charlie was glad
she was on her own. Very few people attacked new cities
the way she did, least of all Karen.

However, most of the warehouses Charlie visited that
day were a disappointment. The proprietors, alerted by
letter that the owner of a prosperous American boutique chain was coming to buy, had eagerly laid out their
most obvious wares—tie-dyes and madras in garish
colors that the Senegalese must have thought would ap-
peal to American tastes, but which Charlie found obtru-
sive and loud. Although most of the men spoke English
very well, it was hard to get them to understand that she
didn't want what most buyers wanted. She wanted
something different, something soft and warm and subtle. She was beginning to feel that her expectations had
been unrealistic when one young shop manager, after
conferring anxiously with several of his peers, nodded
his head and took her aside.

"I think," he said in his precise accent, "that you don't
want to be shopping with us."

"Oh, but I do," cried Charlie, thinking that she had
offended him. "It's just that—"

"No, no, no. I mean you want to shop in the bazaar, I think, where the Senegalese ladies go to buy their fabric. Not the poor village people, I'm sure, but the ladies. They know what is lovely, and I think you will like what they buy."

Charlie's spirits soared. "Yes, I think that will be exactly what I want! Can you show me where to go?"

The man smiled broadly. "I can take you there myself."

And so he did. Twenty minutes later Charlie found herself standing in a dim, low room behind an open-air stall in a crowded market redolent of strong spice and raw meat. But the tawdry surroundings were misleading, for the room was filled with a wealth of fabric, the likes of which she had never seen. There were paisleys in glowing jewel tones, delicately hand-painted designs in subtle pastels and earth colors and linens as soft as silk. There were bold stripes in stiff cotton and Egyptian cottons in deep-hued reds and blues. There were ethereal gauzes and sheers in patterns that defied description. And the room stretched back into endless dim caverns, each alcove holding more delights.

Charlie spent four hours at the bazaar, and by the time she was done she had spent almost half her allotted budget. But the prices she got were fantastic, and the manager of the warehouse, who was obviously getting a decent cut from the sale, assured her that he would be able to arrange for the packing and shipment to Manila.

As it was, she bought so much that she needed two boys to help her carry it back to the hotel. She was planning to arrive in Manila before the bulk shipment, and she wanted to have samples of all the material so that she could go over her plans for each pattern in the appropriate fabric. Also, she hated to part with her purchases so quickly and looked forward to going through them again before packing them away in *Electra*'s cargo bay.

She took a taxi to the hotel and was just staggering up the front steps with her two porters in tow when she bumped into someone in front of her. She almost fell backward down the steps, but a long arm reached out to steady her.

"Charlie? Is that you under there?"

"Bobby! Hello! Give me a hand with my treasures!" She dumped a good portion of her paper-wrapped bundle into his outstretched hands, so that at least she could see in front of her.

Bobby was standing on the steps with Karen. Both of them had obviously just come back from a day spent in the bowels of an airplane. Their clothes were clean, but there was unmistakable grime on their hands and faces and an odor of machine grease in the air.

"What on earth have you been up to? Was something wrong with *Electra*?"

"Oh, no," Bobby assured her as they went into the lobby. "I ran into Karen earlier, and she invited me to take a little tour of the Gulfstream. Boy, Charlie, you should have seen her. That is some machine!"

"Devon would kill us if he knew we spent the day taking things apart and putting them back together," Karen confessed. "Fortunately he spent the day off doing God knows what, and I knew there was no chance that he would show up." Karen grinned. "Poking around under the engine mount is not his idea of a fun day off."

Charlie looked back at the two boys who still held her other purchases. "Well, I've been working hard, too," she said. "I've just bought enough material to last me the next three seasons. And what stuff!" Her eyes glowed at the mere thought of the treasures hidden beneath the rough brown paper. "Listen, why don't you help me bring this stuff up to my room, and I'll give you a show? Some of this fabric is invaluable, and when I tell you what I'm going to do with it you won't believe it. It's really exciting! Here," she added, taking a parcel from one of the boys. "I'll take this, and Karen, you take the other. We'll order lunch in my room and have fun unwrapping presents just like Christmas!"

Her grin was infectious. Karen returned it at once as the boy handed the package to her. "I'll be glad to help you get this upstairs, Charlie, but I think I'll have to beg off the fashion show. I'm none too clean, as you can tell, and I'm pretty beat. I think I'll just grab a sandwich and a nap. We have an early takeoff tomorrow morning, and I want to be rested."

Although the excuse was definitely sincere, and Karen didn't show the least distaste at the prospect of Charlie's "fashion show," Charlie was hurt by Karen's obvious lack of interest. She spent hours listening to Karen talk engine talk—couldn't her old friend spare an hour for Charlie's other passion? Of course, flying and plane engines were an interest both women held, which Karen implied was the only interest worth pursuing. Although Karen had never said as much, Charlie was sure that she thought fashion was superficial and not worthy of Charlie's time.

Charlie dared not to look at Bobby as the three of them made their way up to her room. What if he felt the same way Karen did? Karen's indifference rankled, but Bobby's would wound much more deeply.

Charlie's room was small, and the two guests with their huge parcels made it seem even smaller. Yet she was relieved to note that Bobby made no move to leave after depositing his package next to Karen's on the bed. He went quickly to the bathroom to wash up. Karen, unaware of Charlie's reaction to her decision not to stay, cheerily took leave of them. Bobby sat on the one chair in the room, straddling it backwards. He watched as Charlie closed the door behind Karen and turned to him with a funny smile on her face.

"Well!" she said brightly, coming into the room and looking for a place to sit. "I'll bet you had a nice day, didn't you?" As soon as she spoke, she knew the words rang false. And she hadn't even meant them to! But Bobby's amused smile told her her mood hadn't gone unnoticed.

"We had a fine time," he said with a quick lift of one eyebrow. "But not, I suspect, as nice as you." With a wave of his hands he indicated the mountain of parcels surrounding Charlie. "See? I've washed all the airplane grease off—now, let's see all your treasures."

Charlie felt awkward. She was sure Bobby didn't care one bit about the fabrics, and she was annoyed with him for not admitting that. But she had invited him up, and to renege on the invitation after her initial enthusiasm would have been too obviously petulant. She had to show him what she'd bought.

She began unwrapping the strings that bound the first package, but the twine was too thick for her to manage. She got up to look for a pair of scissors, but Bobby leaned over and ripped the parcel open with one swift pull. Fabric, brilliantly colored, came slithering out onto the bed and the floor.

"Hey!" He bent down and scooped up a handful of cotton paisley, letting it run through his fingers like water. "This stuff is exquisite! What are you going to do with it?"

All at once Charlie's doubts left her. She sprang forward and took the material, draping it across her chest and holding it back around her waist. "See! This is going to be like a caftan, only shorter and slimmer. And this—" she grabbed the next piece of material he had found "—this will make a beautiful shirtwaist."

"But it's see-through."

"Of course!" Charlie lifted the densely patterned chiffon to her face. "But there will be this—" she rummaged on the bed until she found a complimentary patterned piece "—to go underneath. And you can wear the bottom part alone or the top part over a body stocking. Three outfits in one!"

As usual, she was totally absorbed in her enthusiasm for fabric and design. She was unstoppable, tearing off wrapping, seizing one piece after another and delivering plans and patterns, most of which must have sounded like Greek to Bobby. But he sat there, smiling through it all, pointing to one fabric after another, asking questions when he could get a word in edgewise.

"Here," Charlie said at one point when the room was already strewn with enough material to cover a three-ring circus, "hand me that white silk over there, behind you."

Bobby moved to pick up the piece, then hesitated. "I'd better not," he told her. "I'm still not as clean as I could be. Maybe we should take a break, anyway. We never did get lunch you know, and it's almost time for dinner."

Immediately Charlie knew she had made a mistake. Bobby had never wanted to see all that fabric; he had merely been humoring her in his polite Southern way. She was his boss, after all. He could hardly have denied her request that he stay. And she had even forgotten about ordering lunch! She felt her cheeks reddening, and she looked down at the hand-printed linen swatch in her hand. How could she have been so stupid?

"You're right," she murmured. "Sorry I kept you so long."

When Bobby got up from the chair, she assumed he was leaving. She went to the door and held it open for him, unwilling to look at his face. Instead, he reached out and gently shut the door. With the other hand he lifted her chin so that she had to look into his eyes.

"Hey," he said softly, "I never said I wanted to leave, did I?"

"No, you didn't. You're too polite to say so directly."

"Do you think I've been sitting here with you for the past hour just to be polite?" He chuckled. "I'm not that well-bred, Charlie, believe me."

"I'm sure you've been dying to go clean up and rest. After all, you and Karen must have had a hard day together under that engine mount."

Bobby's eyes narrowed as he searched her face for signs of envy. All he saw was hurt. "We did have a hard day. And I'm sure that's the only reason Karen begged off this afternoon. Although I can't say I've missed her, I must admit."

Charlie saw a brief flash of desire light up his eyes, but she didn't respond. "Oh, come on, Bobby. Karen was just being honest. She doesn't think a day spent shopping is as important as a day spent working on a plane—and neither do you."

Bobby pursed his lips. "I think that depends on the in-dividual—and on the situation. The Gulfstream needed work, and that was foremost in Karen's mind. You can't blame her, can you?"

"I don't blame her. I'm asking about you."

Bobby surveyed her steadily for a few moments before replying. "I was happier there than I would have been with you today, yes."

"You see!" Charlie felt bitterly triumphant, fatigue only adding to her self-pity.

"But that doesn't mean I'm not much happier to be with you now," he pointed out. Charlie, however, wasn't listening. All the tension of the day, the effort of maintaining her poise with Bobby and pretending that the special experience they had shared yesterday morning hadn't been important—all that was beginning to wear on her.

"I suppose you think I'm not much of a pilot," she said morosely, feeling as if all her reserves of strength had abandoned her. "After all, I don't spend twenty-four hours a day thinking about flying like you and Karen do."

Bobby went back over to the chair and sat down. He picked up a piece of dark paisley and wound it idly around his wrist. "I have wondered about your divided loyalties," he admitted.

His honesty further inflamed Charlie. "My divided loyalties? Well, what about yours, Bobby?"

He looked up, surprised. "Mine? I have none."

"That's just it!" She exploded in anger. "You can sit there smugly dissecting my divided loyalties, as you call them, and I don't even know what there is in your life apart from flying! I mean, I don't know the first thing about you, Bobby Dupree—what makes you tick besides the fact that you're a great flight mechanic?"

A flicker of anger lit his eyes, but his expression remained mild. "Charlie, I would have hoped you would know more about me than that by now. I thought you did."

"Well, I don't." She couldn't mask the petulance in her voice.

"I don't even know why you chose to come on this trip, do you know that? I mean, really, why? And you still haven't told me why you get so nervous on takeoffs. After all—"

Bobby stood up so suddenly that Charlie stopped in mid-sentence. Something about his posture told her she would be wise not to rave on. But his voice was still soft and drawling. "I told you," he said. "I came on this trip because I like adventure—and because I love to win. And as far as my fear on takeoff goes . . . well, you'll just have to accept it as one of those little quirks—just like I accept your shopping sprees and your fascination for your boutiques."

"Is that all you do?" His choice of words reactivated her anger. "Accept them? Tolerate them—and me—as if I'm some flighty female who can't get down to anything serious on a full-time basis? Is that what you think?"

They stood flaring at each other for a moment, then Charlie saw the anger fade from his eyes, from his face, from his whole posture. "God," he said gently, "that's not what I think at all! How did we get to this state? How could you think that about me? About yourself?"

"You just said—"

Bobby stepped forward and took her by the shoulders, the dark paisley cloth still wound around one hand. "Charlie. Charlotte Frehling, listen to me. I think you are an amazing person. And I know you think—you *want* to think—that I've got some deep dark secrets I'm purposely hiding from you. The sad truth is there's nothing to hide. What you see is what you get, lady. I'm a one-sided, left-handed grease monkey who gets nervous when my plane takes off. There's nothing else to tell."

He spoke with no trace of self-pity, but Charlie was instantly remorseful. "Oh, Bobby, I didn't mean—"

"I know what you didn't mean, honey, and you know what? It doesn't matter. The point is, I think you're amazing because you have two very separate identities. I could never handle what you do—undertaking a race like this and running a business at the same time. The fact that you spent yesterday flying across the ocean and today buying a fortune in fabrics says more for you than my ability does for me, believe me."

Charlie reached out and touched the paisley-bound hand. "Come on, Bobby," she said, feeling uncomfortable in the face of this onslaught of praise. "I'll bet you have a lot of other skills. I know you're not just a grease monkey."

"Oh, yeah?" There was wry humor in his face. "How do you know?"

"I just do, that's all." She looked into his eyes and tried to let him know the truth—that she knew more about Bobby than she could ever say—and all of it had been learned without words.

He seemed to understand, because his expression softened. "Well," he said, "I'm glad to hear you say that, Charlie. I really am. And you're right, of course." He reached up to stroke her face with his free hand. "But I don't have your ability to handle two such separate worlds at once—and both so well." For a moment his expression was gloomy again, and he gripped the paisley, pulling the fabric until the veins in his hand stood out. "I've tried in the past to be a more rounded person. You've got what it takes, Charlie. I've said it before— you're an ace."

Charlie looked at him. He was still gripping the fabric so hard that the blood was draining from his hand, although he didn't seem to notice. He watched her steadily, and she realized that she'd been a fool to jump to any conclusions about Bobby Dupree. He was full of surprises; this intimation of a very private dilemma wasn't the least of them. She couldn't doubt his sincerity, and at once she regretted her self-pitying accusations.

"I'm sorry," she said in a quieter voice. "I guess I was just feeling left out. You and Karen seem to have so much in common, and I...well, I sort of straddle two worlds." He looked up at her sharply, and she hurried on. "I'm not jealous, you understand," she said, wondering even as she said it if that, indeed, had been the reason for her outburst. "I just feel...sometimes I just wish I could commit myself completely to one thing. I feel second best at two things instead of the best at one."

Bobby smiled, relaxing his hold on the material. "You've got to be kidding." He took her hand. "Here you've got twice as much as the rest of us, and you think you only have half?" He laughed a little as he pulled her closer to him. "Boy, Charlie Frehling, have you got a lot to learn."

"That's exactly my point. I *do* have a lot to learn." She looked up, acutely aware of his hand holding hers tightly. "I know I have a lot to learn. I just don't know where to go for my education."

Bobby's eyes didn't move from hers as she spoke, but they changed subtly. First they seemed to grow quizzical, as if he questioned the motive behind Charlie's words. She herself wasn't sure—she had had no intention of challenging Bobby, but her words had definitely come out that way. Now, as they stared at each other, he must have been wondering whether to rise to the challenge. His quizzical look disappeared, replaced by one of warm amusement.

"I think you could do worse than starting right here," he murmured, pulling her a bit closer. "I mean, I don't know what I could teach you about life in general, but there are some other lessons we could start on." His face was moving closer to hers, and once again Charlie felt compelled to meet those warm eyes, that lean and exciting mouth. . . .

"I suspect you could teach me a lot about life, too," she murmured, watching half-hypnotized as his lids lowered and his lips parted expectantly.

"What sort of lessons do you think you could learn from me?" he whispered, still intent on his goal, although he seemed in no hurry to make contact with her eager lips. "You can fly a plane better than I can. You're not afraid of anything that I can see. . . ."

"Oh, everyone's afraid of something. Aren't you?"

"Aren't I what?" His eyes were closed; he was clearly not paying much attention to her words.

"Aren't you afraid of something?" Charlie wasn't paying much attention to what she was saying, either, waiting for his mouth to come down and cover hers. "I mean," she murmured on, "I know you get real nervous when we take off in *Electra*, don't you?"

"Do you really want me to discuss that?"

Charlie realized she had said the wrong thing. Abruptly she opened her eyes at the acerbity in his voice, and found him looking at her with a mixture of defensiveness and irony. His drawl was exaggerated, as it always was when he was irritated. "Is it really important for you to know about my fear of flying right now? Must we have this ridiculous conversation right at this moment?"

Charlie cleared her throat. No, she hadn't really wanted to discuss Bobby's fears—or her own—especially right then. But his attitude annoyed her. "I'm just curious about you, Bobby, that's all. I don't see what's so ridiculous about that, and I certainly didn't mean for you to get so uptight about it."

"Oh," he replied, the irony growing into sarcasm, "but it is ridiculous. Here we are, about to make love, or so I had hoped, since I've been wanting to kiss you and hold you all day, and I thought you felt the same way. Then, just when it seems we're about to make contact, you start again. You want to know why I turn green around the gills on takeoff. You want to know about my relationship with Karen Michaels."

"I did *not* ask you about Karen!" Charlie retorted hotly, but she knew she'd been guilty of thinking the question, if not of asking it. "I don't care about you and Karen," she added without conviction. Bobby's whirlwind changes of mood were beginning to wear on her.

"You want to know everything about me when the truth is—" Bobby began, still angry, then broke off in mid-sentence. He looked at Charlie, who was glaring at him. He let his breath out exasperatedly in a rush, shook his head and laughed dryly. "Will you look at us? Will you listen to me? What in God's name am I doing?" Wearily he rubbed his face. "I'm sorry, Charlie. I really don't know what got into me. Just forget what I said, okay?"

Charlie, who had wanted to forget it from the start, didn't reply at once, and Bobby reached out and stroked her cheek. "Lord, I've really got you confused now, don't I? Well, darlin', I confuse myself, too, sometimes, if that's any comfort."

Charlie sighed. "We're both confused, Bobby. It's all right." But it wasn't all right, and she didn't know how to recapture the romantic mood. All she wanted to be doing at that moment, despite their spat, was to be kissing him. She bit her lip in frustration.

Bobby's hand, still wrapped in the paisley fabric, came up and lifted her chin so that she had to look into his eyes. He saw the doubt in them, and his smile softened. "You confuse me, too, Charlie Frehling. I'm not sure what I expected when I signed on with you, but I sure as hell didn't expect . . ." He shook his head, at a loss for words. "I sure as hell didn't expect you."

Charlie grinned. "Ditto for me." Suddenly it didn't matter that they were essentially two strangers, and that so far the unanswered questions outweighed the answered ones. They smiled into each other's eyes.

"I guess that's what makes us both adventurers—we love surprises." Bobby said, twisting the fabric more tightly, using one end of it to stroke Charlie's cheek. "We both keep on going in spite of what we don't know, or maybe because of it."

The fabric that stroked her cheek was caressing rather than comforting. "You're gonna lose that hand if you keep pulling so tight on that bandage," she said, feebly trying for humor to avoid what was so obviously about to happen between them. She reached out and began to unwrap the paisley bandage from his wrist. But he caught her fingers with his other hand, and she knew she wouldn't be able to ignore the signals flying between them much longer—nor, suddenly, did she want to.

"Can you feel that?" she asked, taking his hand and pressing it lightly.

His smoky drawl erased the vestiges of pretense. "Oh, yes," he purred roughly, already pulling her toward him again. "I can feel it, all right." With his free hand he reached up and traced a slow seductive path from the top of her head, down her cheekbone, his fingers coming to rest against her lips. "What about you, Charlie?" he whispered. "Can you feel it, too?"

"Before she could reply he bent his lips to hers. The kiss was long and deep and thirsty, and it didn't stop at her lips. His entire body was behind it, so that Charlie had to take a step backward to maintain her balance. She found herself pressing against the bed behind her and knew the kiss had been choreographed for exactly that purpose.

"Yes, Bobby," she murmured. "I can feel it, too."

"And it feels good, doesn't it?" He spoke without moving his lips from hers; she felt his words resonating in her own chest as if she had spoken them herself. She tried to reply, but her mouth was incapable of speaking against the hungry onslaught of his. All she could do was nod and burrow more deeply into his arms.

"Then the hell with education," he said, moving his lips down to her throat as together they slipped back onto the bed. "We both know exactly what we want, and this is it."

In answer, she pulled his lips back to hers and thrust her tongue deeply into his mouth, feeling his tongue respond eagerly, possessing her mouth as his hands possessed her hair, her shoulders and her breasts. She wrapped her arms around him, and they floated more deeply into the fragrant billows of fabric, which settled over and around them. The air was filled with the fabric's fragrance, slightly musky and tinged with sharp spices. Charlie felt Bobby pull sheer chiffon from the pile beneath her, winding it round her neck and dragging it sensuously down the open throat of her dress. It was a touch as delicate as a feather and as arousing as the touch of his fingers on the bare skin of her thighs. Reaching up, he undid the clasp that held her hair up, and she heard him sigh as it fell thickly into his hands.

"It's better than any silk I've ever felt," he murmured against her ear, his hands fanning the strands out across the dazzling fabrics. "I wish I could wear your hair...climb into it and cover myself with it all over." He pulled his mouth away and looked at her, his eyes warm and glowing with emotion. "I wish I could climb inside you," he added more huskily, and then his lips covered hers again, this time caressing so deeply that she couldn't breathe except through Bobby.

Once more there was no rhyme or reason, only the intense need for this lanky man, for his mouth and his body and his hands. Charlie slithered among the strewn fabric, luxuriating in the sense and smell of the material beneath her and Bobby above. She was utterly abandoned to sensation; there was no doubt in her mind that she would further abandon herself as her body moistened and heated under Bobby's touch.

"Let me take your clothes off," Bobby whispered raggedly. "I want to see you covered with silks and satins."

Charlie lifted her arms over her head and let him slip off her cotton jersey dress and her bra. She kicked her panties down and nestled into the pile of fabric, watching with half-shut eyes while Bobby removed his overalls.

"We don't want to ruin this fortune in costly fabric, do we?" he said, then fell beside her on the bed, rolling over with her wrapped in his arms until they were both so entwined in material that it was hard to tell where one piece began and another ended.

It was harder still to say where Charlie's body ended and Bobby's began. He was inside her almost immediately this time as if their discussion and the prolonged wait for that first kiss had been all the foreplay he could stand. Charlie was more than ready for him. Once inside her he took his time, moving deliberately so that their bodies rocked rhythmically and slowly in their harem of billowing material. Charlie arched, moving her hips and feeling the luxury of silk below her, the hard beauty of Bobby's loins above. The fabric no longer represented a fortune in fashions to her—it served only as a cloudlike base from which her body surged in ever-accelerating spirals toward ecstasy. Gradually, and in perfect harmony, their bodies began to move faster and in more complex patterns on the now crumpled and strewn material. Then she no longer felt the cloth beneath her; she was airborne, flying tightly within the aching circle of Bobby's arms, flying higher than she had ever flown before.

It took a long time for them to come down from that trip, for the reality of the fabric to reassert itself beneath their moist and tired bodies and for the room to acquire its usual mundane aspect. Evening had fallen, and the room was dipped in shadow, so that Charlie wasn't sure if it was the lack of light or her own satiated mind and body that made it so difficult to move or think. She was aware of Bobby's legs entwined with hers; for the moment he seemed to be asleep. Arching her head back, she could just glimpse his face, his eyes closed, his sensual mouth at rest in a half smile that she would have liked to kiss if she could have summoned the energy to move.

Instead she lay there, smelling the musky elegance of the fabric, wondering what had happened to make her so different from the person she had been before she had met Bobby Dupree. Yes, of course, he was part of the reason she had changed, and the race, the culmination of a lifetime ambition, could also be held accountable.

But Charlie was aware of some deeper sea change within her. She didn't know what this meant, but it had caused her to tell Bobby she had so much to learn. She was only beginning to sense that there was another side to her life that she had ignored until now, a deep emotional side that she had just glimpsed thus far. She wasn't yet ready to pinpoint the feelings. Even if she had understood them, wariness would have made her reject them. She would go on with the race, and go on with her career and the Electra boutiques. But a seed of knowledge had started to grow that frightened her because it was so new, so untested. She knew her escalating emotional relationship with Bobby was partly responsible, but she wasn't sure she wanted it that way. After all, he was still an unknown. She had a life to go back to after all this was over—what about him? Where would he go after the eighth annual circumnavigation of the globe? She didn't want to think about that, either.

Bobby opened his eyes, dropped a kiss on top of her head and rolled over as if to go back to sleep. Charlie knew she had to wake him up and get him out of her room. It would be, she knew, the only smart thing to do.

"Bobby," she murmured. "Bobby, are you asleep?"

"Nope. Just dreaming."

"Bobby. . . it's getting late—we've got to get ready for dinner, and I've got to pack up all this material, and . . ."

She felt his body stiffen into wakefulness. "And you think it's time I left, is that it?"

"I don't want you to leave, but . . ."

"But it's the smart thing to do, right?"

She was startled that he had used the same words she had just been thinking. "I think it would be better if you did," she said softly.

Standing up, Bobby quickly put on his clothes. "You're right," he said, grinning genially. "It is the smart thing to do." It wasn't until he was dressed that he came back over to where Charlie sat on the bed, a layer of opaque batik pulled around her shoulders as a shawl.

"You and I both have a lot to learn about each other," he said, leaning over the bed to give her a gentle kiss on the forehead. "I don't know when we're going to start the real lessons, but I guess we've just got to get a little smarter before we're ready for the advanced course, huh?"

Charlie nodded, although she wasn't entirely sure what he meant. She was beginning to think Bobby's obscurities were a cover-up for some different kind of knowledge, knowledge he possessed and she didn't. It made her uneasy when he talked in riddles.

"I'll tell you one thing," he said, going to the door and giving her a tender salute. "Being smart has its distinct drawbacks. As a matter of fact, Charlie, right now it hurts like hell." He shrugged. "But you now what they say."

"No," she said, surprised at how weak her voice sounded. "What do they say, Bobby?" In spite of her wish to have him leave the room so she could regain her equilibrium, she half wanted him to come back to bed, to grab her so that she didn't have to think at all.

"They say," he replied with a rueful grin, "live and learn. Live and learn."

6

THE THIRD RENDEZVOUS for the race contestants was supposed to be in Marseilles, but while still back in the States Charlie had managed to get the FAI officials to agree to let her stop in Nice instead. The machinations required to calibrate the difference in mileage and time were monstrously complicated, since it seemed the race authorities never did anything the easy way.

But once she and Bobby had left the Nice airport and were speeding along the coastal road to Charlie's favorite pension, she was glad she had persisted in her wishes. She hadn't been to Electra-Nice in quite a while, and she really wanted to get a sense of what was happening there. Also, one of the shop managers had an exquisite eye for design and color. Charlie was anxious to show her some of her newly acquired fabrics and get some feedback on her design ideas for the winter line.

It was also a relief to be away from the other contestants and the constant tension of the race. Although Charlie had managed to do a lot on her own during their short stopovers, she was beginning to feel the need for a respite. They had only twenty-four hours in Nice and were scheduled to make the hop back to Marseilles the following evening. Still, she felt she was getting a vacation.

Bobby seemed to to feel that, too. As soon as they had settled into their separate rooms—Charlie had made a point of asking for two rooms at the desk—he called her and told her to "get gussied up for a night on the town." Charlie was touched and amused by his excitement and curious about what he might have to offer, since she knew Nice far better than he did. But she was pleased by the prospect of an evening spent alone with Bobby without the specter of the race looming over them. She hadn't had such an opportunity with him since they had first met in the hangar at Hancock Field.

She put on a simple red cotton jersey dress, then rummaged in the small package of sample fabrics until she found a length of silk, printed with a dizzying pattern of dips and swirls in bright tones. This she swung low around her hips and sashed on the side, letting the ends trail down in a saucy bow. As she had suspected, the luminous fabric was lovely enough to make a fashion statement even in this unfinished state, and she promised herself not to let her designs get too complicated so that they detracted from the materials themselves.

Bobby met her at the outdoor café just outside their pension. He had a glass of anisette, and he ordered another one for Charlie as soon as he saw her step from the doorway of the building. They sat beneath small, striped umbrellas, staring across the wide avenue at the quay beyond, sipping the heady liqueur and savoring this unexpected moment of ease and pleasure.

"What did you have in mind for our night on the town?" Charlie asked. Bobby was looking very elegant in tan pants and a lighter beige sport jacket worn over a creamy open-throated shirt. He fitted in perfectly with the casual chic of Nice, just as he had with the tropical formality of Caracas.

Bobby smiled at her as if he knew what she was thinking. "Well," he replied, exaggerating his drawl a bit for effect, "I imagine you know all the in spots to visit here in this lovely little town. But when I say a night on the town, I mean exactly that. I plan for us to take several long walks, stopping whenever we find some place or cuisine that suits our fancy. I can't think of a better way for a novice to discover a town, or for a near native to find something new, can you?"

Charlie had to admit she couldn't, adding silently that, with Bobby, anything they did was likely to be an adventure. She had finished her anisette and was beginning to feel a warm glow all through her body, although the sea air was crisp and cool on her bare arms. Bobby called the waiter over and settled the bill in what Charlie thought was surprisingly good French.

"Where did you learn to speak the language so well?" she asked as they left the café and headed toward the quay.

"Oh, here and there," he replied diffidently. Then, acknowledging that his answer was clearly not sufficient, he grinned. "Actually, I had a teacher in the sixth grade who was French. I developed a mad crush on her and basically picked up the language because I used to listen to her as if an angel were speaking directly to me." He chuckled. "I was a hopeless romantic at twelve, you see, but I guess it paid off in some ways."

Charlie would have liked to have told him that as far as she was concerned, he was still a romantic in several enchanting ways, but something about his expression counseled her to silence. Being a hopeless romantic didn't seem to please him in the least.

The clear Mediterranean light was waning into a spectacular sunset, and the pleasure boats that had been out for a day on the water were slowly motoring back into the harbor. Nice was always a festive city, but to-

night it seemed especially charmed. It was still too early
in the season for the tourists to appear in locust swarms,
and so, except for the very rich, whose pleasure knew no
season, the Niçoises had their lovely city all to themselves. Charlie and Bobby wandered along the quay, past
the opulent yacht basin up to the smaller fishing-boat pier
at the far end of the harbor. There they found a tiny
roadside café that looked as if it belonged in the middle
of the countryside rather than in the heart of a seaside
port. They both took one look at the crisp, checked ta-
blecloths, and one sniff of the rich garlicky aroma, and
headed into the establishment without a moment's discussion.

They were right to trust their instincts. The rotund
proprietor, sensing their eager palates, served them huge,
steaming bowls of bouillabaisse piled high with shell-
fish and plump white fish and surrounded by an array
of side dishes. Charlie and Bobby helped themselves to
liberal spoonfuls of the pungent aioli, the garlic-based
mayonnaise that traditionally accompanies such dishes,
as well as downing equally generous quantities of crisp
white wine.

They had meant to dine in small portions at several
intriguing little spots, but by the time they left the quayside bistro they were far too stuffed to do anything but
walk and digest. Bobby asked Charlie if she would take
him by Electra-Nice, but Charlie was reluctant to break
the sweet mood of the evening with a trip to the main
shopping thoroughfare, which she knew would be a
carnival of well-dressed men and women promenading
around and through Nice's most exclusive night spots.
She wanted to keep the pristine beauty of the evening—
and Bobby Dupree—all to herself.

So they walked along the breakwater on the western tip of the harbor and from there were able to turn back and look at the dazzling lights of the city nestled along the shore. The air was cooler near the water, so Bobby took off his jacket and swung it around Charlie's shoulders.

"You don't have to do that. Now you'll be cold."

He smiled crookedly at her in the semi-darkness. "If one of us is going to be cold," he said gently, "better me than you."

Charlie laughed. "You know what you are? You're a throwback, that's what. You belong in another century."

"A throwback?" He feigned a wounded expression. "Now that's a terrible thing to say, Miss Charlotte."

She shook her head at his overripe drawl. "It's not such a bad thing to be. Not if you're a throwback to a better time." She looked up at the starry sky. "And sometimes," she added thoughtfully, "I do believe the old days were the good days."

"Well, now that's an interesting point," Bobby said, reaching up and stroking a loose strand of hair from her cheek. "Did you ever think, Charlie Frehling, that you'd be sitting here like this and saying that the good old days were better than the freewheeling, adventurous life you lead in the here and now?"

She looked at him. "I wasn't really referring to myself, I guess. I mean, I've got it pretty good in the here and now, although I don't really think of my life as adventurous and freewheeling, but now that you mention it I suppose a part of me longs for those old-fashioned virtues of purity, patience and prudence." She laughed at herself. "I've just never really thought about it before."

"But you're thinking of it now, aren't you?" He was watching her closely, and Charlie's eyes slid back to the gaily lit shore. She felt incredibly safe and secure in the darkness, sitting on the rocks next to Bobby. Safer and happier than she'd felt in a long time. "I guess I am. Of course, what I'm saying is silly in a way. If I had lived a hundred years ago I wouldn't have had the Electra shops." She laughed. "And I certainly wouldn't have had our little *Electra* to fly around the world, now would I?"

She looked up at him, but he wasn't smiling. "No, but there are other things you might have had. This night for instance, this place, that wonderful meal. Some things don't change that much. Some don't change at all."

Without being told Charlie knew what he was thinking. Men and women don't change that much either, he had meant to say. The feelings between the two of them right now, as they sat there on the old jetty that jutted out into the Mediterranean, such feelings might have existed a century ago. A man and a woman might have sat together under the stars and fallen a little bit in love.

Charlie was afraid to face feelings of love. For her they weren't enough to go on. She saw herself as a businesswoman, a designer, a flier. What she did—her shops, her designing, her buying trips and her flying—were all a part of who she was. The idea of also being a woman in love had always frightened her. That was why she had never allowed herself to become committed to a man, although several had been eager to persuade her.

Love with Bobby Dupree scared her more than ever because what they wanted from each other was as yet unstated. Already so much existed between them—a wonderful professional attachment, two wild forays into a world of passion she had barely known existed and their deep but undeclared knowledge of each other.

Whatever it was that they shared, it was beyond the realm of ordinary experience. It was only during moments like this that she felt how very real their connection was.

Charlie turned and looked at him, but his face was angled away from hers, back to the glittering shore. In profile Bobby looked older. She could see the lines etched around his eyes and the resolute set of his jaw even in repose. An instant ago she had felt in touch with his every thought and feeling. Now, as if by an effort of will, he had turned his mind and heart away from her and inward to some unknown meditation.

She wished he would tell her what he was thinking—perhaps that would help her to clarify her own muddled emotions where Bobby was concerned. Perhaps he was wishing things could go back to the way they had been, back to that intimate camaraderie that hadn't threatened to develop into an explosive sexual relationship. Charlie thought their journey together would probably go more smoothly if that were the case. Perhaps he regretted embarking on this trip at all, since it may have evolved into more than he had bargained for. Charlie knew it had for her. But she couldn't bring herself to regret being with Bobby Dupree. On the ground and in the air, he was a pleasure.

Suddenly Bobby shivered. Maybe that was all *he* was thinking about, Charlie thought ruefully—how chilly he was! "Hey, now you're getting cold," she chided him.

He turned to her with a slight start as if he had momentarily forgotten her presence. "What? Oh, no, I'm fine."

But Charlie was already standing up. "No, don't be silly. It's cold out here. Why don't you take your jacket back for a while?"

Bobby got up and took her hand with a grin. "Now who's being chivalrous?" But he didn't object to returning as they made their way back over the broad flat rocks to the shore.

"Where to now?" Charlie asked when they had gained the quayside avenue once again. "Would you like to go back to the hotel and warm up with a hot drink?" The idea appealed to her.

Bobby shook his head. "No, I'm fine now, thanks. If it's all right with you, I wouldn't mind walking a bit more." He was silent for a minute, then stopped and turned to Charlie, taking both her hands in his. "If you want to know the truth, I'd like to avoid going back to the hotel until we're really tired." His voice sounded curiously choked. "I'm dying to make love to you again, Charlie, but I know it's not a good idea. So let's just walk until we're too beat to think about anything but sleep, okay?"

He began walking again without giving Charlie time to respond to this amazing statement. Why was he so sure it was a bad idea? she wondered. She wasn't, now that his desire had been so baldly stated. His expression, when he had spoken, had been both ardent and tortured and had aroused Charlie more than she cared to admit.

But there was clearly no room for argument. Bobby was no longer her cordial escort; now he was a man determined that things should go the way he wanted them to. He walked quickly as if trying to leave behind a demon of desire. Charlie had no choice but to walk beside him, stunned into silence by his quicksilver change of mood.

They walked for over an hour, wandering among the empty and silent warehouses and steeply pitched apartment buildings that wound up into the hills. Bobby was

LOTTO PRIZE DRAW
RULES AND REGULATIONS

NO PURCHASE OR OBLIGATION NECESSARY TO ENTER THE PRIZE DRAW

1   To enter the Prize Draw and join our Reader Service, follow the directions published. The method of entry may vary. For eligibility, Prize Draw entries must be received no later than 31st March 1994. No liability is assumed for printing errors, lost, late or misdirected entries and unreadable entries. Mechanically reproduced entries are null and void.

2   Whether you join our Reader Service or not your prize draw numbers will be compared against a list of randomly, pre-selected prize winning numbers to determine prize winners. In the event that all prizes are not claimed via the return of prize winning numbers, random draws will be held from among all other entries received to award unclaimed prizes. These prizes are in addition to any free gifts that may be offered.

3   Prize winners will be determined no later than 30th May 1994. Selection of the winning numbers and random draws are under the supervision of D. L. Blair Inc., an independent judging organization whose decisions are final. One prize only to a family or organisation. No substitution will be made for any prize, except as offered. Taxes and duties on all prizes are the sole responsibility of winners. Winners will be notified by mail. The chances of winning are determined by the number of entries distributed and received.

4   This Prize Draw is open to residents of the United Kingdom, U.S.A., Canada, France, Germany and Eire; 18 years of age or older except employees and their immediate family members of Torstar Corporation, D. L. Blair Inc., their affiliates, subsidiaries, and all other agencies, entities, and persons connected with the use, marketing or conduct of this Prize Draw. All applicable laws and regulations apply.

5   Winners of major prizes will be obligated to sign and return an affidavit of eligibility and release of liability within 30 days of notification. In the event of non-compliance within this time period, prizes may be awarded to alternative winners. Any prize or prize notification returned as undeliverable, will result in the awarding of that prize to an alternative winner. By acceptance of their prize, winners consent to the use of their names, photographs or other likenesses for the purposes of advertising, trade and promotion on behalf of Torstar Corporation, without further compensation, unless prohibited by law.

6   This Prize Draw is presented by Torstar Corporation, its subsidiaries, and affiliates in conjunction with book, merchandise and/or product offerings. Prizes are as follows:-

Grand Prize - £600.000 (payable at £20,000 a year for 30 years).

The First through to the Sixth Prizes may be presented in different creative executions, each with the following approximate values:

First Prize		- £25,000
Second Prize		- £ 6,000
Third Prize	(x 2)	- £ 3,000 each
Fourth Prize	(x 5)	- £ 600 each
Fifth Prize	(x 10)	- £ 150 each
Sixth Prize	(x 1,000)	- £ 60 each

7   Prize winners will have the opportunity of selecting any alternative prize offered for that level. Torstar Corporation may present this Prize Draw utilizing names other than 'Million Dollar Sweepstakes'.

For a current list of prize options offered and all names that Prize Draws may utilise, send a stamped self-addressed envelope marked 'Prize Draw 94 Options' to the address below.

For a list of prize winners (available after 31st July 1994) send a stamped self-addressed envelope marked 'Prize Draw 94 Winners' to the address below.

Prize Draw address:
Mills & Boon Reader Service,
PO Box 236, Croydon, CR9 3RU.

mps
MAILING
PREFERENCE
SERVICE

Mills & Boon invite you to play
£600,000 LOTTO!

324698

LOTTO CARD No: SA

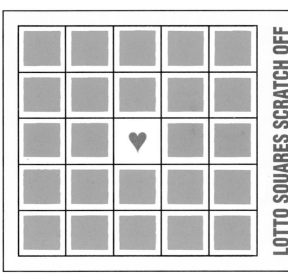

LOTTO SQUARES SCRATCH OFF

Instructions: Using a coin edge, scratch away 4 or 5 silver squares in a straight line (across, down or diagonally). If 5 hearts are revealed, this card is eligible to win the £600,000 Grand Prize: If 4 hearts, £25,000; 3 hearts, £6,000; 2 hearts, £3,000; 1 heart, £600. VOID IF MORE THAN 5 SILVER SQUARES ARE SCRATCHED AWAY.

AND...
YOU CAN CLAIM A MILLS & BOON ROMANCE ABSOLUTELY FREE AND WITH NO OBLIGATION

To register your entry in the draw and to claim your free book simply return this card. Don't forget to send us your address!

DON'T HESITATE - REPLY TODAY!

Mills & Boon

ROMANCE
Love Island
SALLY HEYWOOD

Over190 pages - worth at least £1.70 with the compliments of Mills & Boon

LOTTO REGISTRATION CARD

YES, please register my entry in the £600,000 Lotto Prize Draw. And, please send me my FREE Romantic novel. I understand that I am under no obligation whatsoever.

3A3PD

Ms / Mrs / Miss / Mr _____

Address _____

_____ Postcode _____

Signature _____

Please note that the offer expires on 30th September 1993 and is subject to availability. Only one application per household. Readers overseas please send for postage details. In Southern Africa write to Book Services International Ltd., P.O. Box 2464, Craighall, transvaal 2024. You will receive further information from Mills & Boon about how you can receive more FREE books and gifts.

mps
MAILING
PREFERENCE
SERVICE

NO
STAMP
NEEDED

MILLS & BOON
READER SERVICE
FREEPOST
P.O. BOX 236
CROYDON
SURREY
CR9 9EL

right; this was a Nice Charlie had never seen before, one full of menacing shadows and crowded alleys and the smell of sewage mingling with the briny odor of the sea. She wasn't worried about their safety, however, because they walked as if they had a purpose, and she doubted that anyone would want to tangle with Bobby, given the expression on his face.

She was wrong. Just as they turned a narrow corner that brought the sea back into view, something bounded out of the shadows toward them. Charlie screamed, and Bobby jumped in front of her, his arms raised in battle-ready position. Then they both realized their attacker was a dog, and a small one at that. It was too dark to see the color, but they could clearly hear the threatening growl deep in the mongrel's throat as it blocked their path.

For a moment all three were at a standoff. The dog remained motionless except for the rumbling in its throat, and Bobby stayed in his combative crouch while Charlie stood frozen with apprehension behind him. Then, without warning, Bobby kneeled down and extended his hand to the mutt.

"Here, here," he whispered soothingly, "it's all right. No one's going to hurt you, little fella. It's okay."

Charlie was sure the beast would snap Bobby's hand off, but to her surprise the little dog instantly stopped growling and began to whine. He stepped forward and nuzzled his nose against Bobby's hand, and the whine turned into a curious sort of purr.

"Are you sure he won't bite?" Charlie took a tentative step out from behind Bobby's back.

"Bite? Hell, no, he's scared to death. Poor thing's been badly mistreated." He lowered his voice to a soothing croon. "There, there, it's all right now. We're here. It's all right."

The dog stepped closer into the circle of Bobby's arms. Charlie, who had never been a real animal lover, was surprised by Bobby's behaviour. He seemed to have forgotten all about the tension that had accompanied them like a third person; he was totally absorbed in the animal's shivering delight. Charlie sighed. The man was full of surprises. "Be careful," she warned as Bobby scooped up the dog. "What if he's got some kind of disease?"

Bobby looked at her incredulously. "The only thing wrong with this poor mutt is that he's been abused."

Charlie couldn't argue with that. Seen more closely, the animal didn't look as threatening as it had on the ground. He was nothing more than a mass of bedraggled fur with two big brown eyes sticking out, eyes that now regarded Charlie with a mournful luminescence that melted her heart.

"What are you going to do with it?" she asked.

"I'm going to find it something to eat for starters," Bobby replied as they began to walk back down to the water.

"What if it belongs to somebody here?"

Bobby scowled. "If this dog belongs to someone around here, which I doubt since he has no tag, they don't deserve to get him back. More likely he's been kicking around the neighborhood and getting kicked back by everybody he meets up with. Isn't that right, little fella?"

The animal's tail actually began to wag, and Charlie couldn't help smiling. There was Bobby in his immaculate European suit, loping down the steep cobbled street and holding a mangy dog as if it were his cherished offspring. Charlie's heart melted further toward both Bobby and his canine charge.

They reached the pension, which was dark and silent except for a small light over the concierge's desk. "It looks like the café is closed down for the night," Bobby observed. He turned to Charlie. "Why don't you go on in and get some sleep? I'll try and scout out an open restaurant or store and get this little fellow something to eat."

Charlie hadn't expected to be summarily excluded from this search for food. She was somewhat taken aback, especially when Bobby turned away without a word of farewell.

"Uh, Bobby?" she said, speaking the words softly to his retreating back.

"Yes?"

Charlie smiled at the look of barely concealed impatience on his face. "Good night," she whispered. "To both of you."

Bobby's face broke into a grin. He took two steps back and planted a gentle kiss on her lips. "Good night, sweet Charlie. From both of us."

And then he was off into the darkness.

HE WASN'T AROUND the following morning, and Charlie didn't see him again until later that afternoon. She was at Electra-Nice, sitting with Celeste, her shop manager, amid a cascade of her new fabrics, when they both heard a bright little bark from the front of the store.

"What on earth . . . ?" They turned just in time to see a fluffy white ball charge into the room. The fur ball bounded right up to Charlie and planted two clean paws on her blue-and-white-striped jumpsuit. "What the . . . ?"

The arrival of Bobby, grinning proudly, answered the unspoken question. Charlie looked from Bobby to the dog and back again. "Is this our disreputable mongrel?"

Bobby nodded happily. "Yup. That's the mutt. Quite a change, huh? It's amazing what a bath and a meal can do, isn't it? Or should I say, a bath and three or four meals. Boy, he was one hungry creature, that's for sure."

Charlie chuckled as the dog lapped eagerly at her outstretched fingers. "Well, he appears to recall me as a savior, too, don't you, you cute little fur face?" Then, remembering her manners, she looked up. "Oh, Celeste, this is Bobby Dupree, my copilot. Bobby, Celeste LeGrande, my manager here at Electra-Nice."

Immediately, Bobby was on his best behavior. He came forward and took Celeste's hand to plant a swift kiss on the inside of her wrist. "*Madame*, it's my pleasure," he said in French. "Your shop is every bit as enchanting as you are."

Celeste raised her brows in approving surprise. "Thank you. And who is your little fluffy friend?"

"That," said Bobby with a swagger, "is General Lee, best first steward in the commercial jet business. General, say hello to the lady."

Unfortunately, General Lee hadn't yet learned to be gallant and continued to ignore Celeste in favor of Charlie. But it slowly dawned on Charlie that Bobby had just made an important announcement.

"First steward, did you say?" She looked up quizzically at Bobby, who nodded innocently. "Does that mean what I think it means, Bobby Dupree?"

Bobby took a step forward, and instantly General Lee bounded into his arms. "Well," Bobby said reasonably, "I can't very well leave him here, can I? He'd just end up

the way we found him—or dead." General Lee whined
obediently at this.

"But, Bobby, we can't take him on board *Electra*. The
FAI people would never allow it, not to mention customs."

"Oh, you've handled the FAI people before," he said
confidently. "And, besides, who has to know? I've gotten him all his shots, so he's clean. And I've set up a little
berth for him in the back of the cockpit—if necessary, he
can stay there without being seen when we make our pit
stops."

"Without being seen, yes, but what about being
heard?" Charlie was trying to be patient, yet sensed she
was fighting a losing battle. Celeste looked on with good
humor. "Besides, what about feeding him? And walking him? He can't very well stay on board all the time
without . . . well, without needing some exercise and a
spot of grass, don't you agree?"

Bobby put the dog down. General Lee went right back
to Charlie, this time jumping up into her lap. He curled
up into a little ball and lay there playing possum as if eager to show her just how good he could be.

"Now, Charlie, don't you worry about the General.
I've got the whole system figured out. You can set your
mind at rest. He's coming along, and he's going to be just
fine."

It was clear that the battle, if there had ever been one,
was lost. Celeste shrugged her shoulders expressively,
and Charlie, whose hand had mysteriously gotten caught
up in General Lee's fragrant fur, couldn't think of a single thing to say.

SO IT WAS that General Lee joined the crew of *Electra*,
holing up in a little nest Bobby had built for him behind

the cockpit and behaving as if he had flown all of his little life. Charlie was extremely nervous that night when they left Nice to fly to Marseilles, and even more worried when they left Marseilles for Cairo, but Bobby had been right. No one searched the plane, and General Lee was mysteriously fed and walked without Charlie's quite knowing how this had all come about.

The stopover in Cairo was brief, though Charlie managed to spend another day, and another small fortune, stocking up on fine Egyptian cottons and linens at incredible prices. She was getting more and more excited about her winter line, and she no longer doubted her ability to handle both the rigors of the race and her business. She even found time to check in with Marla back in Baltimore and, over a crackling telephone connection, to help her resolve a few problems.

Charlie and Bobby, it seemed, had worked out an ideal relationship. She handled the actual flying and all her shopping arrangements, while Bobby handled the endless technical checks—and, of course, General Lee. The two fliers had established an easy rapport that, if not quite as straightforward as it had been in the States, at least made for a comfortable working environment. Neither of them brought up the subject of their arrested physical relationship or any emotional attachment. Occasionally Charlie fell into the trap of thinking there never had been an emotional relationship, at least on Bobby's part, that the episode had exhausted a sudden and passing passion. Anyway, Charlie had disciplined herself not to think about personal matters during the trip, and besides, she was so busy that she barely had time to think at all.

The excitement of the race was building to a climax, and the Egyptian tourism board hosted a dinner for the contestants during their short layover in Cairo. *Electra's* standing in the race was more than creditable for her class of jet, and Charlie prepared for the event with a special excitement. She and Karen were planning to share a room at the small hotel, and she was looking forward to catching up on their friendship without mechanic's talk coming between them.

In fact, Bobby didn't show up for the dinner until it was almost over. Charlie wasn't willing to ask him in front of the tableful of fliers where he'd been. She was sure he'd been taking care of General Lee; the collusive smile that passed between them as he sat down across from her was proof positive. At that moment, watching him greet the others and yet save that private smile for her, she felt herself slipping a little bit more in love with him. She was wrong, she decided, to think he didn't have a special place in his heart for her. She wasn't sure yet what that place was, but she knew it existed—a little niche where she would love to curl up and rest for a while, safe and secure.

All during the meal, as Bobby regaled the others with hilarious tales about his adventures on other, nameless journeys, he kept on turning to her and smiling secretly. *Wait*, his smile seemed to be saying, *wait until we're alone. I have special stories for you—stories that only you can hear*.

She was unaccountably aroused just listening to him, waiting for those honeyed eyes to swing around the table to her. Her meal was forgotten as she listened breathlessly along with the others to Bobby's soft drawl and rich laughter. She was waiting for some hidden sign, some private message that tonight might be the night they resumed their exploration of each other's body and soul.

There was the small problem of Karen, but Bobby had apparently been thinking along the same lines as Charlie. As they all moved to leave the table and go into the dark-panelled bar for after-dinner drinks, Bobby stopped by her chair and bent over to whisper in her ear, "I'm in room 408. Alone. The door will be unlocked." He planted a swift, hot kiss on her neck. "God, but I want you!" was all he said, and then he was gone, lost in the crowd of fliers.

Charlie found herself short of breath and weak with arousal. The mere sound of his voice had hypnotized her into a nearly orgasmic state, and she doubted her ability to walk steadily into the next room. Karen, who had apparently picked up on the undercurrents, took her arm just then and grinned. "Come on, kid," she said with a wink. "You look like you could use a little fortification. After all, you have a busy night ahead of you."

Ordinarily Charlie would have tried to deny what was putting that gleam in Karen's eye. But because her friend's reaction was mixed with unmitigated approval, even a touch of melancholy, Charlie couldn't bring herself to deny the obvious.

"Don't worry," Karen went on, seeing her friend's speculative look. "Whatever secret you've got is safe with me. And might I add, you are one lucky couple." She put her hand over Charlie's and gave it a squeeze. "It's inevitable for you two," she said, "so why fight it?"

Charlie leaned forward and kissed her friend. "You're something else," she said with a grateful smile. "You know that?"

"Sure I know. Now let's get that drink, huh?"

CHARLIE BARELY MADE IT through those next few hours. Bobby seemed to be in no rush to escape to his room, continuing his role of raconteur without even glancing in Charlie's direction. But just when Charlie was beginning to doubt that she had heard him correctly, wondering whether she should be embarrassed or annoyed by his delaying tactics, Bobby got up and, with an elaborate yawn, made it known that he was going to bed.

His departure signaled a general lull in the conversation, and soon the rest of the crew was drifting off to separate rooms. Charlie was careful not to leave until a suitable period of time had passed after Bobby's departure, although there was no reason for anyone to be the least bit suspicious.

Finally Karen leaned across the table. "For God's sake," she hissed, "it's going to look weirder if you're the last to leave than if you had left right on his heels. People will think you're waiting for an assignation with the Egyptian secret service or something!"

Charlie jumped up as if she'd been stung, and quickly saying good-night to her few remaining acquaintances, walked up the three flights of stairs to the fourth floor. She felt sneaky and guilty, looking down the corridors before she slipped rapidly across the oriental carpet to room 408.

The door, as Bobby had promised, was unlocked. At first there was no sign of the occupant, and Charlie, feeling foolish about standing alone in somebody else's hotel room, wondered if perhaps she had blundered into the wrong room. God, that would be just her luck!

Then she heard his voice from the balcony. "Out here," he said, and she gratefully parted the linen curtains that led out to a small terrace. Bobby had a room in the topmost corner of the hotel, one of the few with a terrace. The thick whitewashed walls looked out over the old section of Cairo, and the delicate shapes of the mosques and minarets looked like part of a movie set from some past romantic era. Charlie sniffed and caught the scent of eucalyptus and orange trees and saw, in the crescent of moonlight that provided the only light, the silvered tops of the trees sloping down to the Nile banks. It was the most exotic scene.

Bobby, too, looked fairly exotic. He lay on a narrow chaise longue that nestled in the curve of the balcony wall, his face mostly in shadow. But she could see his lean body, clad only in a white waist-to-knee wrap of fine linen that seemed to catch the moon's glow and reflect it back at Charlie. He was completely relaxed, and she thought she could see a small smile on his generous mouth.

"You look like a real native," she said with a slightly nervous laugh.

"Do you like my Egyptian sleepwear?"

"Very stylish. I think I might be able to use you as a model as well as a copilot when we get back to the States." Somehow her words sounded pompous and silly, and although Bobby didn't respond, she rushed to correct herself. "Not that you're not a terrific pilot, of course. And not that you'd ever want to work for me that way. I mean, I didn't mean it to sound like I was...I don't just think of you as an employee. All I meant was . . ."

She trailed off miserably, and Bobby laughed, a deep satisfying chuckle. "I know what you mean, or what you didn't mean, and none of it matters. Do you know what I think?"

Charlie swallowed. His control in this awkward situation was making her feel even more awkward. "What do you think?"

"I think that for all your sophisticated ways, Charlie Frehling, this is the first time you've been in a gentle-

man's hotel room." He lifted one long arm and languor-
ously held it out to her. "Am I right, Charlie?"

"Well . . ." Charlie felt very naive at that moment. She
had always thought of herself as sophisticated without
ever really applying the term to Bobby. Now their roles
were reversed. Though she struggled to maintain her
poise in the face of this reversal, she couldn't ignore the
gentle command in his gesture. "Actually," she said,
moving forward along the red-tiled floor toward the
chaise, "you may be right. I've been—"

"I don't want to know where you've been," he said
sharply. "I just want you to be lying with me right now.
Right now."

Suddenly it was very simple. They needed each other
and were eager to go to any lengths to explore and sat-
isfy that need. With a little sigh she sank down on the low
couch and melted against his warm body. He gathered
her on top of him and fitted her legs to the length of his,
so that their bodies matched, inch for inch, on the narrow bed. Charlie's thin silk dress was almost no barrier
to the heat of Bobby's bare skin, but soon even that was
too much. With their lips welded and the rustle of eucalyptus around them, together they rid her of her dress
and undergarments, a cumbersome collection of re-
straints.

Bobby's attire presented no such difficulty. As he became even more aroused, the flaps of the skirt parted and
fell back, leaving his lean bare flanks to be kissed by the
moonlight. Charlie raised herself off him so that she
could drink in the pleasure of his body, but he was even
then reaching up and licking lightly at her breasts, which
made it impossible for her to support her own weight.
She sank down on him with a groan.

Bobby had told her recently that she had a lot to learn—that they had a lot to learn about each other—and Charlie knew he was right. She was ready to act, confident in her supreme knowledge of his body and what it took to arouse him. Lying on his chest and legs, she dropped her head and traced tiny circles around his nipples with her tongue, letting her teeth follow with intermittent nips against his inflamed skin. She rotated her hips against his until she could feel him hard and insistent, then lifted and dropped her weight in a teasing pattern that made him moan almost angrily into her hair. The strands fell over him in loose sensuous swirls, obstructing his vision and his breath. Yes, Charlie had much to learn in her life, but she had just learned not to be afraid of her strong appetites and desires, especially where Bobby Dupree was concerned.

Her lesson was rewarded when Bobby, uttering an indistinct growl, wrapped his arms around her and, in one smooth gesture, switched positions so that he lay on top of her. She would have liked to have continued her mastery of his body, but Bobby apparently had other thoughts. Using his hands, his mouth, his tongue and teeth and his strong legs to mold her body into the desired positions, he seemed to uncover new regions of sensuality everywhere he touched her. She had never known the flesh on the insides of her arms could be so tender to the touch of his fingertips, or that the outside of her thigh could be stimulated, as well as the inside, by the long hard stroking of Bobby's knees. The soft skin between her ribs was heated by his mouth, and then her loins, until she cried out with the need to have him inside her.

Charlie had never before been so willing or able to abandon herself to sensation as she did that night with

Bobby. She felt paralyzed and yet energized by desire, as if the foreignness of the Egyptian air had affected her brain as well as her body, turning her into an alien being who existed only for the pleasure of touch and the need for consummation. There was no shame, no constraint, and no regret.

Then Bobby was ready. It seemed he didn't enter her so much as they entered each other. Their bodies joined at every possible juncture of flesh to flesh. They clung together so closely that they seemed to merge. They abandoned any semblance of control as they rocked together toward climax. Just at the moment of consummation Charlie heard from the tops of the minarets the eerie wail of the muezzin calling the Muslims to prayer. Odd, she thought, at this time of night.

Then she realized it wasn't the prayer call she heard, but her own high voice, crying out at the height of passion as her body melted into the temple of Bobby's soul.

7

THIS TIME IT WAS DIFFERENT. This time Bobby insisted they spend the night together, and nothing Charlie could say would convince him to let her leave his chaise and, later, his bed. Every time Charlie murmured that she really did have to be getting back to her own room, Bobby would shake his head, smile and cover her lips, or her breasts, or her abdomen with his mouth, so that the last thing she wanted to do was protest....

She sensed that this time their lovemaking had been different in other ways, too, not just because they spent the night together, although that in itself signaled a new level of intimacy. There was something greater growing between them, something neither could yet openly acknowledge. Every once in a while during that long and passionate night, one would catch the other's soft smile of amazement. It was tacitly agreed that those smiles didn't require an explanation, but at least once they had led to a bout of lovemaking that was remarkable for its slow, tender affirmation.

Charlie knew what was happening—she was beginning to feel deeply committed to this man. And this frightened her, not only because she could not be sure that he was equally involved, but because she herself wasn't ready for the change. Commitment meant caring and changing one's life to accommodate another and questioning one's priorities—all things Charlie hadn't had to deal with in a very long time. The fact that her future with Bobby was so tied up in the race and in *Electra* didn't make the mess easier to sort out.

It was a complicated night, blending passion, humor and private insecurities into a dreamlike mix of pleasure and near pain. Charlie would have been content to ride the ever-changing moods of that dark Egyptian night all the way to morning, but Bobby insisted they get some sleep. "The real race begins tomorrow," he told her, gently kissing the top of her forehead as he tucked the thin cotton sheet around her bare shoulders. "Much as I'd like to make love with you forever, we do have a big bout of flying coming up, and it won't do to have either of us groggy from lack of sleep."

Despite herself Charlie nodded, smiled and immediately dropped off into a deep and restful sleep. She dreamed only of the darkness of the Egyptian sky and the fragrance of orange and eucalyptus. And she dreamed about flying, although for the first time in her memory she didn't fly in *Electra*, but freely on her own gossamer wings through the night.

The next morning she woke up to find Bobby sitting naked on the bed beside her, holding a tiny cup of steaming black coffee.

"What time is it?" she asked, sitting up quickly, her hair spilling forward and covering her breasts.

"Relax. It's only five-thirty." Bobby held out the coffee to her. "Drink this before you go. There's plenty of time to get back to your room before the rest of the crews start stirring." He smiled and reached out, lifting the shiny brown hair from her breasts. The mere brush of his fingers against her bare skin was enough to arouse Charlie; her nipples sprang outward as if eager for his caress. Bobby, although his eyes grew soft with desire, shook his head. "Oh, no, you don't, lady. You and I both know there's no time to start that again—not if we want to do it justice, which is the only way I can think of to make love to you. We've got a race to think about, right?"

Charlie cleared her throat with a sip of scalding coffee. "Right," she replied, trying to sound sure of herself.

Bobby's eyes roved back to her expectant breasts, heaving slightly and glowing in the light of the just-risen sun. He sighed mightily. "I just wanted a last look," he said, then got up and walked quickly into the bathroom. In a minute Charlie heard the shower running and took that as her cue to get up and dress hastily. Rather than waiting for Bobby to reemerge, she scrawled a note and pinned it to the pillow. "Hate to drink and run," it read, "but we both have a date with a Lear jet." She thought of adding a "thank-you," but decided that would sound too condescending. Anyway, she couldn't bring herself to say anything else that might reveal the emotional turmoil the night had stirred up. She knew the note was almost cold in its brevity, but she hoped he would understand.

As Bobby had promised, Charlie encountered no one on her way back to the room, and Karen was still deeply asleep. Charlie managed to slip into the shower and into a serviceable lightweight jumpsuit before Karen stirred and lifted her head sleepily off the pillow.

"When did you get back?" she asked. "I never heard you come in last night." She sat up and rubbed her temples as if to rid herself of the sleep that clouded her brain. "I don't usually sleep so heavily," she added.

Charlie decided not to tell Karen that she had returned only twenty minutes ago. The two women finished their preparations, and by mutual consent they talked about the race and not about Charlie's relationship with her copilot. Charlie wouldn't have traded one minute of her time with Bobby, but she regretted not spending time with Karen. Karen, however, distracted by preflight anxieties, didn't comment on how little they'd seen of each other. They had coffee and a large breakfast together in the room, going over the flight plans as they ate. Cairo was to be the last real stop until Calcutta, a good three thousand miles away, and that would only be an eight-hour layover. The planes were scheduled to make a refueling stop in Bahrain, but neither *Electra* nor the Gulfstream would get into the next port until early the following morning, and the flight from Bahrain to Calcutta, mostly a night trip, was generally thought to be one of the more difficult legs of the journey.

For some reason Charlie wasn't the least bit nervous. Her confidence as a pilot, and in *Electra* and Bobby, had grown with every leg of the race thus far. She had no reason to suspect any of them would do less than their best at clocking good time. She felt the thrill of adventure tingling in her stomach but no feeling of tension at all.

Such was not the case with Bobby. As soon as she saw him, standing with a group of men in dark jackets outside the terminal of Cairo's main airport, she knew he was wound up in knots. And before she even reached the group, she realized why.

General Lee was in his arms, looking bedraggled and forlorn. Charlie felt a sudden constriction around her ribs. How had the little mutt gotten out? It was clear he hadn't spent the night in his doghouse on board *Electra*—his fur was damp and his paws dark with mud. He wagged his tail slightly when Charlie approached but didn't seem to hold out much hope for his own salvation.

"What's going on here?" Charlie asked with as much authority as she could muster.

Bobby turned to her, his expression not unlike General Lee's. "They've found the General. He got out of the plane somehow, and the night crew saw him." His jaw tensed. "The FAI officials don't want him on board. They say it's not allowed, according to the rules governing the race."

"Well, that's just ridiculous," snapped Charlie. "What can a tiny dog have to do with the outcome of this race?" She glared at one of the officials, who spread his hands and shrugged.

"Don't look at me, madam," the gentleman said in heavily accented English. "I'm not with the FAI. I'm with Egyptian customs."

"Oh? And what does Egyptian customs have to say about the matter?" she inquired coolly. Charlie knew she was taking a risk in asking this. It was possible that customs would be even more adamant than the FAI about General Lee's not leaving the country. But she was in her element in situations like this. The thing to do was to put the attacker on the defensive and make him clarify his position. Invariably, as she had found in her dealings with suppliers and manufacturers, the attacker's position softened.

The man shrugged again. "Well, as far as Egyptian customs is concerned, the dog is cleared to leave the country. He had the proper immunization certificate when he came in, and we have no quarantine procedures here for properly inoculated domestic animals. But I can't promise you the same treatment in your other ports. Some countries will automatically quarantine the animal for as long as six months—others will not accept the certification as valid. You're really taking a chance."

"But that's up to us, isn't it?" Charlie favored the man with a swift, dazzling smile, and he nodded submissively. She turned her attention, but not her smile, on the others. "So. There seems to be no immediate danger to world health here, according to the Egyptian customs officials—whose decision I assume you gentlemen are willing to accept."

The FAI officials quickly glanced at the Egyptian customs man and assured him that they did not doubt his ruling on the matter of the animal's suitability to travel.

"Then what seems to be the problem, gentlemen?" Charlie knew she was winning the battle, and she allowed herself the smallest of wide-eyed smiles. Behind her she could feel rather than sense Bobby's growing elation, and General Lee seemed to have picked up on the turn of events, too, because he snuffled happily in Bobby's arms.

"The problem," said one of the men, stepping forward somewhat reluctantly, "is that there is no provision in the race rules to allow for a pet on board."

"No provision to allow for it? Ah." Charlie put her hand on her chin and pretended to be thinking. "Well, but that means there might also be no provision in the rules prohibiting a pet, am I right?"

The man looked stricken. "Well, yes, but that doesn't mean—"

"I don't care what it doesn't mean," Charlie said quickly. "I'm only concerned with what it does mean. Does it, or does it not mean that there is no rule expressly forbidding domestic animals as cargo?"

"Cargo?" The official cast a withering glance at the General. "You call that cargo?" He pulled himself up for a last-ditch attempt. "Miss Frehling. Since the inception of this race—*before* the inception of this race—we have constantly been bending and reshaping certain rules and regulations for your benefit. I don't know who was responsible for allowing you to carry actual cargo on this trip, but I assure you that if it had been up to me, I would have refused. There was also the small matter of your making an unscheduled stop in Nice rather than flying to Marseilles like the rest of the crews. I suppose you feel that, being a woman, you are entitled to extra considerations from the FAI, but I, for one, shall see to it that you get not one more concession from me!" He shut his mouth tightly in triumph and took a step back among his peers.

Charlie eyed him speculatively until she was certain that all eyes were upon her and not on him. Perhaps, she thought with private glee, they were waiting for her to burst into tears. Isn't that what men like this usually expected women to do in times of stress? But they hadn't figured on Charlie Frehling!

"Well," she said with apparent finality, "I suppose that's your final word, then, isn't it?" The man nodded vigorously. "I can have no concessions beyond the ones already granted me by the American and French FAI officials, is that it?"

"That is absolutely it, Miss Frehling."

Charlie waited a moment for the tension to build. Then she turned to Bobby and scooped General Lee out of his arms. "Well, then, that's settled. Come on, General, let's get you tucked back into the cargo bay."

She turned to leave the little group while Bobby, who had already figured out her game, walked beside her.

"Wait just a minute!" thundered the official. "I just said—"

Charlie turned. "You just said I could only do what had already been accorded to me by previous negotiations. And that's exactly what I'm doing."

"But you've only been cleared to carry cargo!" the man objected.

"Cargo! That's exactly right. And General Lee is cargo. He stays in the cargo bay from now on, is that clear, Mr. Dupree?"

"Clear as the day is long," drawled Bobby laconically, although his eyes were bright with laughter.

"But that dog is not cargo. What does he have to do with your dress business?" The official was beginning to panic.

Charlie allowed her wide-eyed, innocent look to go full force. "Oh? Didn't you know? My designs are famous all over the world. I use dog fur as trimming for all my best gowns. You should see the poodle trim on last year's wedding gown—what a smash hit that was!" She smiled graciously at the dropped jaws and horrified expressions of the men before her. "But don't worry, gentlemen," she added soothingly. "I've decided to hold my fur budget down this year. I think General Lee will be all I'll need for my winter line—won't you, you little fluff ball?"

And nuzzling her head into General Lee's neck to muffle her laughter, she linked her arm through Bobby's and walked away toward *Electra*.

"You won't get away with this!" the man shouted after her. "You'll never even get that dog into the next port!" Then, when he saw that his words had no effect, he added, "I hear they *eat* dogs in Calcutta!"

"Great!" Bobby threw over his shoulder. "As long as they save us the pelt, we'll be fine! So long, y'all!"

IT WAS A GLORIOUS WAY to start the trip; even Bobby was too delighted to be noticeably nervous on takeoff. "Boy," he said, shaking his head admiringly, "you really handled those guys like a pro."

Charlie wriggled her eyebrows at him and grinned. "I am a pro when it comes to dealing with people like that."

"When aren't you? A pro, I mean." They had reached twelve thousand feet, their cruising altitude for a while, and there was time to talk, even though Bobby and Charlie both kept their eyes focused on the blue sky.

Charlie thought for a moment before answering. She would have liked to have referred to their night together, and to the feelings it had aroused in her, and she still felt bad about the brief note she had left on the pillow. "I suppose I come off as amateurish when I'm in a situation that's out of my control," she said, trying to keep her voice light. "When I don't know what to expect from the other party—or from myself. That man down there was totally predictable. Sometimes it's not so easy."

She looked sideways at Bobby, but he appeared not to have picked up on the on the personal implications of her speech. *So*, she thought, *he's playing it cool again*. She understood why. This was race time, not personal time. Both of them had too much invested to let themselves be distracted. Yet she couldn't suppress a pang of regret, because Bobby was so clearly engrossed in his work and so obviously unaware of her dilemma.

The only way to deal with this situation, she decided, was not to deal with it. As the afternoon wore on she found it easier to concentrate on her job and not on her copilot. The flight from Cairo to Bahrain was over desert and thus fairly uncomplicated. But she knew that once they were in the sky again, they would be flying across the entire Indian subcontinent, and they would be much more subject to capricious wind shears and weather factors than they had been during the Atlantic crossing or over the Red Sea.

The stop in Bahrain took longer than they had expected. They had agreed that it would be simpler not to produce General Lee for this short stopover. Somehow, Bobby managed to smuggle him out for a brief walk and a meal, but he was tense all the while, and the fact that they were hiding the animal from Bahrainian officials didn't make the stay any easier. For the first time Charlie felt a twinge of apprehension. What if something did go wrong? They had a long flight ahead of them, albeit not as long as the Recife to Dakar flight. If they had to go down on land, where would they do so? *Electra* was equipped with all the modern safety measures, but an emergency landing on the ground was risky business. General Lee's presence did nothing to ease her nervousness. She almost wished she'd given in to the Cairo FAI officials and let him stay behind. After all, he was Bobby's dog, and she wasn't sure she wanted to put her flight in jeopardy for a tiny mutt.

Still, it was Bobby who seemed far more tense about the trip than she did, and she found herself resenting that, too. All he could talk about was the race—where they stood in it, how the other planes were doing, what they could do to save time. Although Charlie didn't say anything, she was irritated by his single-minded concentration on the competition. Was that all he really cared about—winning and his dog? As they waited endless hours for clearance from the Bahrainian airfield, she had to restrain herself from reminding Bobby that if he hadn't taken the time to care for his precious General Lee, they might have saved some precious time. She knew the shot was unworthy of her, so she stayed quiet.

Nevertheless, the atmosphere in the little cockpit had changed. Both pilot and copilot were laboring under real pressure, but there wasn't time to reflect on the causes for that pressure. Bobby's competitive spirit was infectious, and Charlie, even though she would have liked saying she was only in the race for the love of flying, knew she felt the same way he did—she wanted to win. She just wished she could be sure Bobby wanted something else besides winning. That he wanted her as she wanted him.

Thinking about it afterward, Charlie thought their moodiness almost portended disaster. They were about five hours out of Bahrain, just over the northwest part of India, when they sensed trouble.

At first there was only a slight drag on the right side of the plane; Bobby noticed it before Charlie did because he was sitting on that side. He looked out his window and pursed his lips.

"Hey. Did you notice that?"

"Notice what?" It was twilight, and they were just about to gain landfall. Charlie was concentrating on her visual flight rules.

"That drag. It feels like—" He broke off and bent over to examine the instrument panel more closely. "No," he decided, straightening up, "it couldn't be. The altimeter doesn't show anything and neither does the compass."

"Doesn't show what?" Charlie hadn't felt anything yet.

"Well, nothing, I guess. I just thought there was a little—" The plane gave a slight jolt, clearly noticeable this time, although *Electra* seemed to right herself at once.

Quickly pilot and copilot looked at each other in the dimming light of the cockpit. "What *was* that?" Charlie asked.

Bobby took a deep breath and shook his head. "I'm not sure yet. At first it felt like a slight wind drag to the starboard side. But that was more pronounced than drag."

"It felt as if we hit something," Charlie said. They both turned to peer out the windshield on all sides. The sky was a pale smoky grey with a hint of darkness creeping forward over their heads as they flew east.

"Or something hit us," Bobby added. He twisted in his seat to look back at the engine on his side, then twisted to survey the instrument panel once again. "Maybe it was just a—"

Suddenly the plane bucked powerfully, and the right engine failed. Bobby lunged to grab the yoke and help Charlie to resist the compensating force of the left engine, which would throw *Electra* into a rotary spin if not corrected. The starboard engine monitors registered the failure, and the altimeter began to drop accordingly as they fought to keep the plane on an even keel.

Charlie looked over at Bobby, her eyes wide. Was it just the green light from the control panel that gave him that sickly look, or was Bobby as scared as she was? No, though he usually did turn several shades paler on take-off, he seemed perfectly calm and in control—under the circumstances. His aplomb boosted Charlie's confidence. "What do you think it is?"

"From the look of things—and the feel of things—I'd say some kind of external interference. It's not a vapor lock from the engine itself, and it's not a pressure problem or an electrical problem—we'd see all that. The left engine is clearly not getting enough oxygen, though, and that's why she keeps stalling out and refiring." That was exactly what was happening, making it even more difficult to handle *Electra*.

"What do you suggest we do?"

"I think we should cut the power entirely and go on to one engine." He looked speculatively at Charlie. "Do you think you can bring her down on one?"

Charlie nodded without hesitation. She had no real fears about her ability to fly the plane as long as she was flyable, but she needed some instruction on what to do technically. "I'm game if you are," she said, forcing as brave a smile as she could muster. "But where are we? Do you have any idea?"

Bobby shrugged. "Somewhere just northeast of Bombay, according to the charts and the compass readings." Bobby checked his measurements and peered out the window again. "We've gained land, if that's any comfort. I'll see if I can raise Santa Cruz Airport in Bombay on the radio. We've been out of contact for too long, anyway. They should be within range by now." He reached out and gave Charlie's shoulder a brief squeeze. "You just bring her down gently, Captain, and I'll find us a place to land."

Charlie grinned wanly and turned all her attention to the task. It wouldn't be easy to bring down an unbalanced load like *Electra* into a dark and alien territory. She had made an emergency instrument flight-rule landing before over Baltimore, but that had been different because she was so familiar with the terrain. Now, even though she still had visual flight capacity, she seemed to be flying into a dark void.

She didn't panic. Fiercely, she concentrated on keeping *Electra* on a steady descent pattern. The only consideration she gave to the where and when of their landing was to offer a brief and silent prayer of thanks for the fine evening weather. The last thing they needed was a sudden squall or a wind shear.

Soon she could make out the terrain below. There was no light, which told her she was far from any decent-sized city that might have a landing field. On the other hand, there were no sudden mountain peaks looming up ahead of her, and her instrument panel told her the ground altitude was fairly level for almost fifty miles in each direction. Another reason to give thanks.

"I've got Bombay," Bobby told her, lifting off the earphones he'd put on so that Charlie wouldn't be distracted. "They say we're about a hundred miles east-southeast of Karachi, which is on the coast of Pakistan. There's no real landing field out here, but they say there's an old RAF dirt strip about twenty miles due east. If we get down to eight hundred feet we should be able to find it with no trouble."

They exchanged knowing looks. If there was any real danger in their situation, it would come during the landing when they had no way of knowing what might rise up in their path. Charlie cut the engine and dropped to eight hundred feet and then lower. All they could see was dark green foliage. She dropped lower, and the pattern of trees and undergrowth became a bit clearer, but the descent was still touch and go. An old dirt strip might be easily missed, especially in the deepening twilight.

"There it is!" They both saw it together, about five miles to their right. Charlie banked steeply, gauged the condition of the strip and circled it in order to come in at a more advantageous angle. A break in the forest left enough light on either side of the strip so that her vision was unobstructed. Still, Bobby stayed on the radio and got precise descriptions of the terrain from the Bombay control tower, so that by the time *Electra* bumped to a landing, Charlie had been informed of every rise and dip on the three-hundred-foot strip.

Bobby told Bombay they had landed safely and that he would check the engine and radio for help if he couldn't fix the problem. Then he rang off and turned to Charlie, who was leaning her head back and waiting for her heart to stop pounding.

"That," he said with a soft whistle, "was some pretty nifty flying, Ace."

Charlie turned to him and smiled wearily. "You know what they say—a pilot is only as good as her crew."

"Where do they say that?"

She chuckled. "In Charlie Frehling's Book of Golden Rules." For a moment they just smiled at each other, savoring the small victory they had just won against the fates. Then Bobby leaned slightly forward in his seat, his face only inches from hers. In the dimness of the cabin she could see the light in his eyes, compelling her to part her lips and close her eyes to receive his kiss. In the barest instant before their lips touched, a sudden sound made them shoot apart.

It took them both a minute to realize General Lee was barking piteously from his home in the cargo bay. Bobby jumped up to rescue him, and Charlie, her former animosity forgotten, leaped to his aid. They released the General from his cozy perch and opened the door so that they could all step outside into the cool night.

They found themselves in a pleasant glade surrounded by medium-sized trees and thick underbrush. The moon had just risen, casting a silvery light over the clearing. Both Charlie and Bobby stood gratefully and silently, taking several deep breaths of fresh air. Then Bobby went to the other side of the plane to check on the engine, while General Lee wandered off in search of a suitable tree.

Charlie followed Bobby around to the left engine and found him halfway into the opening of the intake port. She could see the yellow glow cast by his tubular work-light. "Find anything?"

"Oh, yeah. I found something, all right." Bobby withdrew his head from the intake. "But it's not something you're going to want to look at."

"What? Is something seriously wrong?" Fear stabbed through her as she looked at his pale face.

"No, it's not serious. At least, not for us. But it was pretty serious for the large bird that got into this intake port."

"A bird?" Charlie's eyes widened. "A bird caused all that trouble? I've only heard stories about that happening."

"His detour could have been fatal for us, but he got lodged sideways and didn't block the intake vents completely. That was why we kept on refiring as the engine got intermittent blasts of oxygen."

"So what do you do?"

"Do? Scrape the poor thing off the vents and get back up there. There doesn't seem to be any damage to the engine block, the vents or the wing brace, so there's no reason why we couldn't just clean her up and get along."

Charlie came forward. "Great. Let me help, and we'll get it done faster."

Bobby shook his head. "Uh-uh. Thank you for your bravery, ma'am, but you've done enough for one evening. This, as much as I hate to say it, is a man's job."

Charlie started to protest, but Bobby was firm. "No, you listen here," he said in his most imperious drawl. "I don't say that very often, but when I do you'd better listen, because I am not gonna change my mind. Now why don't you go on into the cabin and cook us up some grits or something like that? I won't be a minute."

Charlie giggled at his lunacy, but let it pass. She was not exactly thrilled by the prospect of pulling bird pieces from the air-intake vents. Her time could be better spent preparing food, although the closest thing they had to grits was a bag of rice chips to go with the sandwiches that had been provided for them in Bahrain. She set out the meager picnic and wandered around the clearing to stretch her legs, waiting for Bobby to finish.

It took him a lot longer than he'd expected—over an hour—before the engine was completely clear and able to fire up without missing. By then both of them had no appetite and wanted only to be in the air again. They had already lost precious hours, and Charlie could tell Bobby was concerned about their standing in the race.

It wasn't until they were almost ready to leave that they remembered the General. "Where is he?" Charlie asked, peering around the clearing as if he might materialize to answer her query.

"He ran off in this direction," Bobby said, and walked to the edge of the clearing calling the General's name. There was no response.

"Why don't you walk out for a ways and call him?" Charlie suggested. "I'll take another direction. We can circle the glade."

Bobby stood still for a minute as if listening for a telltale sound. Then he turned and began walking toward the plane.

"We've got a plane to fly," he said, not meeting Charlie's eyes. "Let's get in and start her up."

Charlie was stunned. "But what about ... ?"

"He's been gone for over an hour. If he doesn't show up by the time we're ready to taxi out, he stays behind."

Grimly he forced a smile. "At least he won't starve around here."

Charlie couldn't believe this was Bobby talking so callously about his adored pet. Bobby, who had risked their participation in the race altogether in Cairo to save General Lee. Bobby, who had sneaked out on his hands and knees to a patch of tall grass with the General so that the dog could take care of business. This Bobby was willing to leave the General behind without even searching for him?

"Don't be ridiculous," Charlie said, and started off in the direction the dog had gone. "He can't be too far away—there's nowhere for him to go, and besides, there's plenty to keep him occupied around here. Why don't we just—"

Bobby grabbed her elbow and turned her roughly back to him. "No! We won't waste any more time on that dog, is that clear?"

"But Bobby—"

"Is that clear, Charlie? He's made life hard enough for you already, and we're too far behind to risk the race because of some sentimental attachment to a mutt. You've got a business rendezvous in Calcutta, and if we don't get off the ground soon you're going to miss that, too."

Charlie simply stared at him. "Is that what you want? To leave the General behind so I can make my appointment? I don't believe you, Bobby." What she didn't believe was the total about-face he had made in the past few hours. This was not the Bobby Dupree she knew—this wasn't even one of the many sides of the man that she had encountered thus far. This man was hard, and Bobby Dupree had never been hard.

Yet his eyes glittered like gold nuggets, and his jaw was set. "That's not all," he said tightly. "I've got a stake in this race, too, you know. I've got something to prove, just like you do, Charlie."

"What do you have to prove? And what makes you think I'm only in this to prove something?" The night air had gotten chilly, and the thicket of green surrounding the airstrip seemed to threaten more than it protected. Charlie shivered. Bobby noticed and softened his voice.

"It's not that I don't care, Charlie," he said. "It's just that I want to be sure we keep our priorities straight. You've put too much into this race—and so have I. We can't jeopardize the whole thing because of some stray I picked up. I won't let you do it."

So that was it. He was blaming himself for the General. But it was the General who would suffer, even more than Bobby would. "Bobby, I won't let you do this. It's not fair. I don't begrudge you General Lee, and I don't think it would be fair to him to leave him here."

"Why not? He'll be fine—better than he was in Nice, that's for sure." Bobby seemed quite confident; Charlie couldn't tell if his reaction was forced. "So come on, let's get going. We've already wasted more time talking about him than he deserves."

He moved ahead of her and climbed up onto *Electra's* wing step. Charlie, unable to think of a single argument to convince him, followed more slowly. She considered walking away and looking for General Lee herself— Bobby couldn't leave without her, that was certain. But the clearing had become ominous, and besides, she felt foolish holding out for a little dog's sake when its owner wouldn't do the same. With a last longing look back at the trees, she climbed aboard.

In silence the two of them went through their pre-flight checking procedure. Charlie tried to move slowly, but Bobby was working with quick precision. She couldn't hold him back. They got the electrical system checked out and revved the first engine, then the second. They were ready for takeoff.

They never would have heard him over the sound of the engines, so General Lee did a very intelligent thing. Instead of running up to the wing step, which was at the side of the plane and out of the view of the cockpit, he bounded to the front and began leaping high in the air. It was Charlie who saw him first, and she shouted to Bobby over the roar of the engine. "Look!"

The look on Bobby's face convinced her that his act had been one of foolish bravado. After one glance he bounded out of his seat, ran around to the front of the plane and caught the excited mutt up in his arms, throwing him high into the air before holding him in what must have been a suffocating bear hug. Then Charlie saw Bobby look at the General, taking something out of his mouth and throw back his head in laughter.

In a moment he was in the cockpit, General Lee in his lap. Charlie looked at both of them fondly and smiled. "That's some smart little critter you've got there, Bobby Dupree. How do you suppose he knew to come around to the front? He's never seen the windshield before. How did he know we would see him?"

Bobby laughed and nuzzled his face against the dog's. His relief was palpable; he filled the cockpit with his energy. Charlie understood what it must have cost him to decide to leave the General behind, and her heart went out to him. She didn't really understand why he'd done it, but the gesture had been well-intentioned—and largely for her.

"You think *that* was smart?" Bobby turned a grin on Charlie. "Look what he dug up out there. He must have found an old RAF cabin in the undergrowth somewhere." He held up a metal oblong tin with barely de-cipherable writing on it. The tin looked as if it had been buried for decades.

"What on earth is it?"

Bobby laughed and went to work on the container. "What do you think? It's old emergency rations left over from God knows what war. It's..." He held a brown package aloft. "Chocolate bars!"

8

THEY WERE EVEN LATER than expected getting into Calcutta's Dum Dum Airport. The clear evening air gave way to dense fog somewhere over the middle of the continent, and it took all their combined attention to fly through the gusting winds and thick cloud banks. It was nearly morning when they finally landed, over six hours behind schedule.

Some of the planes in the race had already landed and taken off again. Charlie and Bobby felt the sharp sting of regret as they saw *Electra*'s standing slip inexorably backward. But there was no question of leaving again without having the intake vents thoroughly cleaned and checked and without getting at least a few hours sleep before the next long lap to Manila, some nineteen hundred miles farther east.

After taking care of their flight debriefing—and finding, to their added dismay, that General Lee would have to be quarantined in the airport kennel during their brief stay—Charlie and Bobby checked wearily into the hotel provided for them, trying to ignore the excited faces of those well-rested fliers who were already checking out. The competitive spirit was reaching fever pitch as the race entered its final and most grueling phase—the Pacific crossing. But neither of them could muster anything more than a dull sense of defeat as they lumbered to their rooms for a few hours' sleep.

They met again in the hotel lobby after only four hours—already it was midmorning, and the short rest had sharpened their anxiety to get back up in the air. But the mechanical checkup still had to be taken care of. Neither Bobby nor Charlie had wanted the official crew to work on the little plane in their absence.

"Look, Charlie, I have an idea," Bobby said. Charlie noticed that he still looked haggard, and that for once he hadn't bothered to change his clothes, although he had showered and shaved. She imagined that she didn't look much more chipper despite her fresh peach-colored jumpsuit and newly washed hair. "I think you should stay here and get some buying done while I take care of *Electra*. They don't need both of us out there, and I know you were planning to get some fabric here."

Charlie shook her head. "Bobby, I can't do that. There isn't time. And besides—"

"Besides nothing. You have enough time to go to one or two of the places on your list, don't you? And you really can't afford not to shop here. Isn't India home to the most fabulous silks in the world?"

Charlie smiled wanly. She had been looking forward to buying silk in Calcutta, a city famous for its vibrant-toned, paper-thin fabric. She had set up appointments with several of the city's best wholesale houses, but even as she spoke she had already missed two of these meetings. "I can always come back another time," she said with resignation. "It's really too late to get anything accomplished."

Bobby shook his head firmly. "If you wait you won't be able to get anything in time for the winter line. We've come halfway around the world. I insist that you take advantage of the situation."

"But Bobby—" She felt tired again, too tired to argue.

"No buts. Don't you think I can handle the tech crew?"

"Of course I do."

"And don't I know more about the mechanical aspects of flying that plane than you do?"

"Yes, you do," she said with a sigh.

"Well, then!" Bobby smiled, and the fatigue lines disappeared from around his eyes. "I certainly couldn't do half as good a job shopping for silk as you, so I suppose we're both stuck with our respective tasks, sexist as that may be."

Charlie had to laugh. "I suppose so." Bobby was right. There was no reason for her to be standing there while he and the crew went over *Electra* with a fine-toothed comb; she would only feel in the way, even if she wasn't. She looked out the window into the street, which was teeming with color and life. Everything seemed to be tinted a lovely saffron orange, the reflection of the sun on the warm stucco buildings. The color gave her a new design idea, and she bit her lip speculatively.

"Well, I can see that's settled." Bobby stood up and clasped his hands in a satisfied gesture. "Give me your bag, and I'll take it out to the plane. That way you can come straight out with your booty, and we can get on our way."

She looked up at him gratefully. "Thanks, Bobby. You're a prince."

He smiled down at her. "Takes a real princess to know a prince," he replied, then bent down and kissed her gently on the top of her head. "Buy something lovely, Princess—something especially marvelous in the lingerie line." He paused, and his tongue licked his lips. "Get something I can take off you—very slowly."

For a brief moment his golden eyes smoked with passion, and Charlie felt the familiar weakening heat rush up from her thighs into the pit of her stomach. Before she could respond to the eroticism of his remark, he tipped one finger to his brow in a smart salute and was gone.

She took a moment to collect herself before she, too, got up to leave. Technically their rooms were theirs until that afternoon. The FAI officials had allotted eight hours to each contestant, although few actually had that much time to spend sleeping. Charlie had no intention of returning to the hotel—she had a lot of work to do and little time in which to do it.

SHE SHOWED UP for her third appointment at a small wholesale house, located in the section of town where the Ganges River ran into the Bay of Bengal. Riding through the streets, Charlie wondered how so many people could manage to live together in such close quarters. She knew to expect unimaginable poverty, but she was surprised by the riot of color and the almost festive air of the people, who gathered in great crowds along the banks of the river.

As soon as she was taken to the storeroom by the smiling manager, Charlie realized she had made another lucky find. She might have wasted hours in the other larger houses before discovering the quality this concern offered. Arranged along the cool, dim walls in rows that seemed to recede upward into the darkness was bolt upon bolt of soft, sheer silk. Charlie walked around the perimeter of the room, running her hands along the fabric. She felt as if she were touching flower petals and, indeed, there seemed to be a tender floral fragrance in the air.

The material was not inexpensive, but again Charlie bought more than she had planned to—it was just too lovely to pass up. Several times she recalled Bobby's erotic command to buy something lovely that he could take off her, and it was difficult not to look at the sensuous colors and liquid patterns without thinking if this piece was right, or perhaps that.... Charlie's face would heat up, and she would lean her forehead against the cool silk until the moment had passed.

It was unnecessary, as well as financially impossible, to visit another fabric house, but Charlie still had an hour before she was to meet Bobby at the airport to prepare for the next lag of their flight. She stood for a moment in the offices of the wholesale house, trying to think of someplace else she might want to go—Bobby, she intuited, would not want her around until everything was shipshape. She could find a place to eat, or visit some shops or just take a walk. But the lack of sleep was beginning to wear on her. Her usual enthusiasm to explore a new city had deserted her. Instead, she would have her packages sent on to the air terminal and then go back to the hotel and take tea in her room.

Later, Charlie could only believe that fate had played a role in her decision, not simply fatigue and the wish to keep out of Bobby's way. The chances were good that the hotel, knowing she had left even if the room was technically hers until that afternoon, had already given it to another guest. Charlie went anyway, and just as she was walking through the door, she heard her name being called.

It was the hotel page, an Indian boy dressed in a satin outfit of brilliant yellow. She approached him with a puzzled air, and he handed her a handwritten message. "Call Bahrani Hospital, extension 409. Urgent."

Charlie glanced wildly at the boy, but he was no help, since his English was nonexistent. All he could do was point to the house telephone, and Charlie ran over to it.

She had only one thought in her mind—Bobby was
hurt—something had happened to Bobby.

She dialed the number and waited interminable minutes until an English-speaking physician could be found,
biting her lips to keep the tears of panic at bay. If Bobby
was hurt, that meant the race was over for both of them.
But it meant far worse than that. If anything happened
to Bobby... Charlie was stunned at how the mere
thought of such a possibility made her weak with hor-
ror. She had known for a while that he meant far more
to her than she had ever expected him to, but this—this
sheer terror at the possibility of life without him! She
couldn't bear the thought, nor the fact that she was so
overwhelmed by emotion.

It seemed an eternity before the doctor came to the
phone. As soon as he said, "Hello," Charlie yelled into
the phone. "What's wrong with Bobby?"

There was a moment's baffled silence. "I'm
sorry... Bobby? I'm afraid there's been—"

"What? What happened to him?" If the doctor had
been in front of her, Charlie would have grabbed him by
the lapels and shaken him out of his dense confusion. Her
harsh words were incomprehensible to the man on the
other end, whose consternation only increased.

"Him? Bobby? I'm afraid... is this a Miss Charlotte
Frehling?"

"Of course it is!"

"From the United States?" His slowness was madden-
ing, but all Charlie could manage was a strangled moan.
"Miss Frehling," the voice went on patiently, "I believe
we have a friend of yours here. A Miss Karen Michaels—"

"I *know* you have a friend there! What I want to know is—" Charlie stopped as the doctor's clipped words became clear to her. "Karen? You have Karen?"

"Yes. Miss Michaels is here." This time the patient tone sounded slightly strained.

"My God!" It was taking Charlie a minute to switch gears. It wasn't Bobby. That was good—that was wonderful. But Karen! "My God," she breathed again. "What happened?"

"She was brought in early this morning with a very high fever. The man who brought her in, a Mr. Devon, could not stay with her. He said he had to leave, and that we should get in touch with you, Miss Frehling, if things got worse." He paused. "I'm afraid they have gotten very much worse, Miss Frehling."

Charlie swallowed back a wave of nausea. "How bad?" she croaked.

"Miss Michaels is in a light coma."

Charlie gripped the telephone cord as if it might lend her support. "What . . . what's wrong with her?"

"It appears she has contracted some kind of virus either in South America or in Dakar. Some sort of tropical disease for which she neglected to get the proper vaccination, although we haven't isolated the strain as yet. Now it's possible that she could pull out of this coma by herself at any time and not need any really specialized treatment. But it appears . . ."

She could not bear to hear any more than "it appears." "I'll be there as soon as I can," she said. "Tell me where you are."

The doctor gave her instructions and rang off. Charlie stood very still for a moment trying to collect herself. Then she dialed the airport, an arduous procedure that took precious minutes. She was put through to the private terminal and told that Mr. Dupree couldn't be reached unless he was in the building, which he most assuredly was not. This time making an effort to control her impatience, Charlie finally managed to clarify that this was an emergency and that Bobby should meet her at the Bahrani Hospital as soon as he could.

Everything in India seemed to be moving at a snail's pace, Charlie thought as her taxi made its way through the crowded streets. What had earlier seemed a delightfully exotic mélange of colors and smells now struck her as a seething mass of humanity, unstoppable, unpassable, as it wound through the narrow streets like a huge amoeba. She found herself weeping silently as the old car coughed and sputtered along at a crawl. Mostly she cried for Karen, but Charlie was aware that she was miserable partly because she understood something for the first time. She was hopelessly in love with Bobby Dupree, and it didn't occur to her that that love could lead anywhere except to heartbreak.

Finally, she arrived at the hospital and located Karen's room. But the door was locked, the small window in the center of the door covered from within by a dirty looking cloth. Charlie pounded on the door in frustration, and a dark man in a white coat emerged at last.

"Miss Frehling? I am Dr. Mehta. I know you are concerned for your friend. Come and sit in the lounge with me, and I will try to explain her situation to you while we have a cup of tea."

Charlie was grateful, both for his placating manner and the offer of tea. She allowed him to lead her into a small but sunny room where a pot of tea warmed on a single burner. He brought her a steaming mug and sat beside her while they drank.

The effects of the tropical virus had come on slowly, it seemed, so that Karen hadn't been aware of any symptoms until it was too late to get a vaccination to modify the effects of the disease. Dr. Mehta couldn't prescribe specific treatment because the bug hadn't been isolated, so Karen had slipped into a coma. Her fever still remained quite high, but her vital signs, though weak, were stable. Did Miss Frehling know, the doctor wondered, how to get in touch with Miss Michaels's next of kin?

Charlie had begun to feel more relaxed until she heard that last question, at which point the fear came surging back. She was trying to recall where Karen's hometown was—Karen's mother, she knew, had died several years ago. Then Charlie remembered that the Michaelses lived in Chicago, where Michaels Aviation was headquartered, and was about to ask where she could go to put through a call to the States, when shouting from the hallway startled them both.

"What do you mean I can't see her? I've got to see her!" The voice was familiar but so tight with panic that it took Charlie a moment to realize who it was. "I want to know what the hell is going on in there, and if you won't let me in, I'll get in without your permission—so help me!"

Bobby! Charlie rushed out into the hallway, where Bobby was being forcibly restrained from entering Karen's room by at least five orderlies. His face was as white as a sheet, but his eyes blazed like molten gold. He didn't see Charlie at first and continued battling his captors, who seemed to be losing ground by the minute. "You fools," he hissed, "don't you understand English? I've got to get in there! I've got to see Charlie!"

"Bobby!"

The single word froze all of them in their absurd tableau. All eyes turned to Charlie, but it took Bobby several seconds to realize she was standing in front of him and not behind the forbidden door. Then he broke free with a mighty shove that sent two grown men sprawling, and he swept Charlie up in an embrace that literally took her breath away.

"Charlie! Are you all right?" Charlie could barely manage a nod in response. "I thought...they told me...the phone call..."

"I called...the wrong message...not me...it's Karen." Charlie had to gasp out the words, but she made no effort to pull out of his embrace. Being there at that moment was too wonderful for her to want to move.

The message sank in. "Karen?" He didn't let her go but held on less tightly so that her words weren't muffled against his chest. "What's wrong with Karen?"

So the whole story had to be explained again, and Bobby had to ask the same exasperated questions Charlie had asked. What exactly was it? What could the doctors do about it? What was the prognosis?

Sadly there was little that could be done at the small, crowded hospital. The lab was almost nonexistent, and the nearest lab, in downtown Calcutta, would probably take weeks to get the results back to them. Their best bet, Dr. Mehta told them, was to get their friend to a larger hospital that would be better equipped to handle her case, preferably out of Calcutta.

By this time Charlie and Bobby had unwrapped themselves, although Charlie still retained a very clear sensation of Bobby's body pressing into hers like a brand. Neither of them discussed the fact that he had gone crazy when he had thought Charlie was ill. Now that he knew Karen was the patient, he was distraught but in control. Charlie understood all of Bobby's reactions perfectly, having run the same gamut of emotions herself when she

had thought Bobby was ill. And she thought she understood what their reactions might mean. Even now, as
they began calmly discussing their options, there was a
special look in his eyes, a look that said, *Yes, I feel it, too,
I know what just happened. But now is not the time to
discuss it.* Charlie, feeling and knowing the same thing,
was content to wait.

"The first thing we've got to do is get in touch with Mr.
Michaels," Charlie said. "I know where he lives."

"In Chicago. I know." Bobby was distracted by a sudden angry thought. "That bastard Devon. Why didn't he
stick around to be with Karen? He must have known it
was serious—how could he just take off like that and
leave her here to—" He broke off with an oath.

"We can deal with Devon later," said Charlie, putting
a hand lightly on his arm. "Right now we have to get
Karen out of here. But where? And how?"

They looked at each other and smiled ruefully. Of
course. There was only one way to get Karen quickly and
efficiently to a better hospital—*Electra.*

"It'll mean a lot of extra time," Charlie whispered.

Bobby nodded. "It'll probably mean the race."

Charlie nodded back. "But we have no choice, do we?"

He shook his head. "No choice at all."

While they were discussing the details of Karen's
transport with the doctors and putting through the
phone call to the States, Charlie and Bobby couldn't meet
each other's eyes. It was as if, having decided they had
no choice in the matter, each had to silently mourn the
hopes dashed, the dreams diffused. Charlie had known
how important it was to Bobby that they do well in the
race, although she was beginning to suspect his reasons
went far beyond those he'd given her. More than just
professional pride and a healthy competitive spirit drove

Bobby. Now the race was no longer within his grasp—
no longer within hers.

What really surprised her was her own deep disappointment. She had joined the race for the love of flying
as well as to win. Only now did she realize she had
wanted to win as much as Bobby.

Still, there was little time to mourn or to examine her
motives or Bobby's. While Bobby discussed logistics
with Dr. Mehta, Charlie put through the call to Alan
Michaels. It was still early morning in Chicago, but she
reached him at his office.

Charlie had known Karen's father slightly from her
high school days. Several times while on vacation she
had visited the Michaelses' baronial Chicago Heights es-
tate. On rare occasions Mr. Michaels would be in town
when the two girls were together. So Charlie was prepared for his brusqueness and his harsh pragmatism in
this crisis. What she hadn't expected, remembering Kar-
en's stories of her father's utter preoccupation with his
business at the expense of his family, was the quaver of
emotion threading through his rapid-fire questions and
no-nonsense commands. Clearly his daughter's emergency had deeply affected the multi-millionaire aeronautics magnate, no matter how he tried to control
himself.

"Where do they say is the best place for her to be?" he
asked Charlie after he'd gotten all the essential information.

"Well, Dr. Mehta says she could pull out of the coma
at any time, in which case she wouldn't need special
treatment. But if it's a rare tropical virus, she'd need to
get out of Calcutta. He says there's an excellent inten-
sive care unit in the Bombay hospital."

"I want her out of India," he replied tautly. "Where else?"

"Well, there are good hospitals in Southeast Asia, I'm sure, but I suspect the nearest good place for her would have to be Hong Kong. There's a very large international hospital there, Dr. Mehta says, and they deal with unusual diseases all the time. The doctor says he personally knows of two excellent people in the field there to whom he can refer Karen."

As she delivered this information, Charlie felt her heart constricting against her ribs. Of course it was the most efficient and desirable plan that Karen be taken to Hong Kong. That was where the best available care was, which was all that mattered. But Hong Kong meant the end of the road for the race. Even if Charlie and Bobby dropped Karen off and left for Manila, they would be too far behind to ever catch up. The FAI would probably disqualify them for the unscheduled stop. The rerouting also meant that Charlie wouldn't be able to deliver her fabric samples to Manila in time to beat the deadline set by her factory manager.

Not that they had any choice. Even when Alan Michaels offered to fly out at once and pick his daughter up, Charlie knew she couldn't accept his suggestion.

"That will waste too much time," she told him. "We're already here, and we can have *Electra* ready to go as soon as Karen is ready. Why don't you meet us in Hong Kong at the International Hospital?"

Mr. Michaels didn't bother to thank her for her offer. "How soon can you get there?" he asked.

"We're ready, but it may take some time before we can get . . . before the doctors release Karen. There are arrangements, they say, and a lot of red tape."

'Don't you worry about red tape. You just hold tight over there. I'll make some phone calls on this end, and you be ready to leave as soon as you hear from me, do you hear?"

Charlie knew he was being brusque rather than rude, and that his nerves were speaking for him. She rang off and went to report back to Bobby.

"He says Hong Kong," she told him in a low voice, and they both exchanged silent glances of mutual condolence.

"Hong Kong." Bobby nodded. "I'll go tell Dr. Mehta to start the ball rolling." He reached out and cupped Charlie's chin in his fingers. "You look beat, sweetie. Dr. Mehta says we can use the room next door to this one to wait in privacy. There's a phone in there, so we'll be able to get Michaels's call when it comes through. Why don't you go in there and try and get some rest?"

"I don't think I can rest, Bobby."

He smiled and stroked her cheek with his thumb. "Try. I'll be back as soon as I'm done, and then I'm going to try, too."

With a nod Charlie let herself be led to the room and given a soft kiss on the forehead before Bobby went down the hall to talk to the doctor. She looked around at the hospital bed, at the tiny dresser and pasteboard clothes chest, at the high, narrow windows covered with flimsy cloth. Sitting wearily on the bed, which was the only place to sit in the room, she thought, *What a way for a romantic odyssey to end, here in a dingy hospital room in Calcutta, with nothing to show for the trip except a cargo bay full of material that I can't make into dresses in time for the winter season.* She plucked woefully at the much-mended hospital sheets and bit her lip to prevent self-pitying tears. Once she started she doubted she would be able to stop.

But that wasn't all—not really. She had something to show for her trouble, after all, didn't she? She had Bobby, or at least she knew now that she loved Bobby. And if his display of panic in the hospital corridor had been any indication, he felt much the same way. It was just that now was scarcely the time to establish a commitment— not when so much had just gone so wrong—not when they were sitting in the room next to Karen, who lay comatose with a possibly fatal disease.

Charlie didn't realize she had lain down and closed her eyes until Bobby came in and gently sat down on the bed beside her. "Everything's set for now," he whispered when she opened her eyes. "Dr. Mehta is waiting for Mr. Michaels to call his office—he'll have the call transferred to this room. And he's given orders that we're not to be disturbed until then. We have a lot of flying ahead of us. We should try to rest."

Charlie smiled and made room for Bobby to lie beside her on the high, narrow bed. "You realize," she said as they lay side by side looking up at the cracked blue ceiling, "that with Karen aboard we'll be dangerously overweight?"

Bobby nodded. "We'll have to leave something behind if we want to reduce risks."

Charlie swallowed and nodded. "Fabric. Have you loaded the Calcutta silks into the cargo bay yet?"

"They're right in front."

"I'll call the ground crew at the airport and have them unload it." She took a breath. "Since I'm not going to make it to Manila on time, I might as well have it stored until I can get it shipped." She swallowed again to remove the lump in her throat.

"I guess." The room was silent for a minute, and then Bobby turned to face her. "Are you terribly sorry?"

Charlie looked at him, started to say "no," then decided to be honest. "Terribly," she replied softly, and he wrapped his arms around her so that she could nuzzle against his chest.

"I know how you must feel," he said into her hair. "You've worked so hard to make everything go smoothly, and now, through no fault of your own, it all goes awry."

"You must feel pretty bad yourself," she said, feeling better simply because of the contact of her cheek with his chest through the open neck of his overalls. "You really wanted to win this race, didn't you?"

"Of course. Win or at least show them how well *Electra* can do. Didn't you?"

"Uh-huh." But somehow, lying there in Bobby's arms, the sting of loss wasn't so bad, neither for the race nor for the winter line. She felt drowsy and melancholy mostly.

Bobby's fingers were thrust up into the hair at the nape of her neck, stroking her sleek head beneath the drawn-back strands. Again, they lay for a while without speaking, and gradually Charlie was aware that his fingers were moving down to her neck, wandering aimlessly along her shoulder and collarbone and carving soft curlicues of sensation into her bare skin. For a while it felt lazy and good, and then it just felt good, and then it began to feel more than good. Charlie pulled her head away to look up into his eyes.

"Charlie," he murmured, smiling down at her with his warm honey eyes, "I know this is neither the time nor the place, but there's something I have to tell you."

She stared at him, trying to decipher his intent. "There's no time or place like the present," she said cautiously.

He nodded. "You're right. And that's my point. You're so exactly right, Charlie Frehling . . . sometimes it scares me to think we met by accident."

"By accident?"

"Well, yes, in a way. When I stopped in to see Jim Sullivan at the airfield that day, I had no intentions of looking for a job—and certainly not for a job as a copilot on some crazy wild-goose chase. As a matter of fact, I had just sworn off flying forever. My plan was to get a job as a short-order cook, a busboy—anything to get me away from airplanes for a while."

"But why?"

"Why? Because I'd had enough. Because I'd been drifting for too long. Because . . ." He sighed, and Charlie could feel the sigh reverberating through his body. "I had a lot of reasons, but they're not important now. What was important was that Jim told me about the job and, when I turned it down, sent me to have a look at *Electra*." He laughed. "He said he just wanted me to check her over for him, see what I thought. He must have realized I'd come across you."

"Do you mean . . . ?"

Bobby pursed his lips. "I don't know what Jim had on his mind. I only know that as soon as I saw you all my plans went out the window." He reached out and gathered her closer; he seemed to be steeling himself to say something difficult. "I wonder if Jim guessed that as soon as I saw you, I would know."

"Know what?" Charlie's heart was beating so fast that she was sure Bobby would feel it against his own chest. She sensed what he was about to say but was afraid she might be wrong. "What did you know as soon as you saw me?"

"Why, that I loved you, of course."

He said it so simply, so easily, that Charlie wasn't sure she'd heard him right—maybe her own eager mind was playing tricks on her. But no, he was going on. "Of course, I had to play the devil's advocate with myself, tell myself it was just an infatuation. But the more time I spent with you, the more right you seemed. Everything about you . . . the way you look, the way you walk, the way you fly a plane—it was all just right." He reached down and tipped her face up so that he could look into her eyes. "I'm deeply and hopelessly in love with you, Charlie Frehling, and I'm sorry if this is the wrong time to say so."

Charlie's eyes filled with tears, and she looked up at him for a long while before she could bring herself to reply. "Somehow, Bobby Dupree," she whispered, "I think you picked the rightest moment in the world. I love you, too."

Their lips moved slowly together and pressed into a kiss that was at once deeply passionate and exquisitely gentle. Charlie exhaled with a huge sigh of relief as if the answer to that one question—did Bobby love her—was all that she'd been waiting for for weeks and weeks. His heart was beating against hers, and it seemed a foregone conclusion that their hearts should beat in perfect harmony.

It took a while, but gradually their kisses went beyond a simple, serene confirmation of love. Charlie wanted more—more affirmation, more commitment. But the narrow hospital bed in the tiny room next to Karen's didn't seem like the appropriate place. She pulled her lips from Bobby's and looked anxiously at the door.

Bobby grinned. "I already locked it," he whispered. "There's no time or place like right now, remember?"

"But what about Karen? I feel . . ."

"Karen," said Bobby as he gently began to unbutton her shirt, "would heartily approve."

He was right, of course. And, even if he wasn't, Charlie had no intention of arguing the point. Now was the time, now was the place to confirm what she had known in her heart for so long. This was the seed of knowledge that had taken so long to root in her mind, the lesson she had been so unwilling to learn. She loved Bobby Dupree, and he loved her.

Slowly and carefully they stood and undressed, more because the event was momentous for them than because they felt the need for stealth. Charlie didn't take notice of her clothing as, piece by piece, it slipped to the linoleum at her feet. She was more intent on watching the well-defined ridge bisecting Bobby's chest, underscoring the muscles that separated his ribs from his stomach. She had seen him naked before—why had she never exulted in that brazen beauty as she did now? She could almost taste the smooth, salty expanse of skin that covered his breastbone, feel the hard knot of his nipple in her teeth. Her lips parted at the thought, and then, when her eyes slipped down to the soft thatch of hair between his legs, she caught her breath impatiently.

"Wait," he said, his drawl accentuated by controlled desire. "Wait, my love, until the moment is right. Let me watch you unfold before me first."

Swallowing hard, Charlie slipped her bra and panties off, and stood trembling in the harsh light of the little room. It was incongruous, but the room seemed as perfectly suited to the moment as a chapel would have been to a marriage. She stood before him, naked and expectant, as proud of herself in her bare and silky skin as she would have been in a white lace dress.

Then Bobby took two steps and gathered her gently in his arms, his hands stroking the curve of her spine, coming to rest on the roundness of her buttocks and working upward along her sides until he cupped her breasts. Dipping his head, he kissed one and then the other, moving back and forth until, at a tender prodding sigh from Charlie, he took one nipple into his mouth. The soft suction of his cheeks and tongue on the sensitized skin made Charlie's legs buckle, and if his arms hadn't instinctively tightened, she would have fallen. He lifted her onto the bed instead, lying down alongside her on the narrow white sheet and running his fingers slowly along her flank, waiting, waiting for the moment to be right to continue. For a long while they just lay there, drinking in each other's love with their eyes, their faces only inches apart. Soon they began to caress each other once more, giving each gesture its full meaning and weight. A touch on the breast, a soft venture between the legs—each motion was a conviction, each sigh of arousal a commitment.

Soon the touching of bodies with hands was not enough, and they moved to be closer with their lips and mouths, maneuvering on the tiny cot as if they had all the room and all the time in the world. Although Charlie could never remember having been so aroused, she placed each kiss, each nibble and tender bite chastely. She moved between Bobby's legs, and he between hers, both savoring the give and take of their intimacy with quiet desire. The room itself seemed to buzz with the expectation of their consummation, but still they followed their stately and silken dance of courtship and acceptance, paying due homage to every inch of naked flesh, every opening to the soul.

Bobby reached down and pulled her up against him, his mouth salty sweet against hers, his breath warm and uneven. The moment could be prolonged no more. "I want you inside me now," she whispered. "I need you to love me."

"I do love you," he moaned, and he maneuvered his body between her legs, into her already warm and inviting interior. Still he moved as if he were handling fine, thin porcelain and not a strong, ardent woman. Charlie knew that he moved with reverence, because for him, as for her, this was a first, a commitment to what they had heretofore denied. They didn't need to "make" love, because they had already created it between them.

This was only the physical articulation of that love and, because it was a deeper commitment than anything they had shared before, so it seemed that Bobby penetrated more deeply into Charlie's body and soul than he ever had before. Had his mouth not come down to cover hers, she might have cried out in pain and pleasure from the depths that were being newly plumbed by his desire.

They moved slowly and in perfect unison to climax, never missing a moment of each other's growing ecstasy. Then the purely physical aspect of their union accelerated of its own accord, and their bodies delved deeper and faster together, rising to blinding heights of sensation. Charlie buried her face in the heated flesh of Bobby's neck, biting him lightly just above his collarbone to keep from crying out. Bobby's head hung over hers, and she could hear his teeth grinding together, his lips against her hair, in an effort to keep back the hoarse cries of ecstasy. The dingy little room seemed to recede into a blank wall of light, but their attention was so riveted inward on each other that they might as well have been a million miles away. The heat from their fused bodies was tropical, fragrant and exotic. They became not two separate human beings, but a single nearly animal entity bent on containing an orgasm that, if allowed to erupt, would explode their universe into a billion fragments of light and heat.

When it was over they lay very still, clinging to the wet pathway their bodies had forged, waiting for the world to subside around them. Their breathing stabilized, and soon the quiet in the room was almost absolute. Neither one of them said a word—nothing had to be said. They simply lay there, utterly spent and content, waiting for the phone to ring with news about Karen.

9

THE CALL CAME about three hours later, just as Charlie and Bobby were drifting into a light sleep. They had spent the ensuing time—after dressing to prevent any embarrassing intrusions—lying side by side on the bed, talking quietly about themselves and the life they might have together. During that subdued time, when all the crises that had precipitated their current situation seemed to have faded into the twilight, Charlie and Bobby felt there was no barrier to their future. They discussed endless outrageous possibilities as if they were the most practical options in the world—Charlie would open a sportswear factory; Bobby would help her run it and they would travel around the world buying and selling fabric to other designers; they would sell the Electra boutiques and open a flight school; they would move to Australia and raise sheep—whatever they mentioned rang with truth because they were newly in love.

The phone call put everything into perspective. Whatever else they did with their lives, the present was accounted for in ways they couldn't have foreseen. They were out of the race, for all intents and purposes, and Charlie had missed her deadline in Manila, which was as good as saying her entire deal with the factory was off. Beyond that, they had the task of transporting Karen safely to Hong Kong—a job they both knew would be as difficult as it was pressing.

They met Dr. Mehta at the door to Karen's room. Alan Michaels had done what he could to cut through the red tape, but he hadn't been able to avoid all the bureaucratic delays and burdens of such a delicate operation. Not only did the hospital have to give a special release, but the local officials insisted on having a paramedic travel with the group to insure that, in the event of a medical emergency en route, the Calcutta hospital wouldn't be blamed.

Neither Charlie nor Bobby bothered to point out that *Electra* was already overloaded. This was no time to create more difficulties than already existed. Somehow they would have to manage. And their first sight of Karen, pale and seemingly lifeless on the stretcher as she was wheeled out of the room into the corridor, was another harsh reminder that they had no choice.

They did discuss one thing—General Lee. Bobby, of course, wanted to leave him behind.

"That's absurd, Bobby," Charlie pointed out wearily. "Why?"

"Don't we have enough to worry about without him aboard?"

"Why should we worry about him? He's no problem. He only weighs ten pounds with his traveling cage—God knows an extra ten pounds won't matter now." Charlie looked at Karen with her battery of heavy medical equipment and at the woman who was to accompany them. Impulsively Charlie reached out and took Karen's hand—if only she would wake up, right now! If only she would open her eyes and smile and ask how long she'd been sleeping. That would be so like Karen to return to consciousness with a wry comment. Then everything in the world would right itself, and everyone could go on with his or her life.

But there was no sign of life in the waxen face, and the fingers she held were lifeless and cold. Charlie shuddered, closing her eyes against a sudden rise of panic.

Bobby reached out and squeezed her shoulder. "You're right," he said softly. "Another ten pounds won't matter. Besides, we could use a little liveliness on this trip. The General is one rescue mission that worked. Maybe he'll bring us luck." He kissed Charlie gently and went to make a phone call to see that the General would be delivered to the plane on time.

They made a sad little procession traveling through the crowded city to the airport. The ambulance carrying Karen and the paramedic had to stop constantly for traffic, and Charlie felt the seconds slipping by for Karen as acutely as if the sands of her own life were running out. At the airport they had yet another series of delays, which an angry phone call from Alan Michaels only exacerbated. The Indian customs officials, although they had already been informed of the impending departure of a comatose patient, insisted that everything be checked thoroughly in case goods were being smuggled out of the city. That was when Bobby began to lose his temper, and it was only Charlie's restraint and the surprising diplomatic skills of Mira, the paramedic, that kept the scene from escalating into a major confrontation.

Fortunately General Lee had already been cleared for passage, so there was no struggle on this account. When they finally got to the plane, he bounded out to meet them with such pure glee that their spirits lifted considerably. Charlie was glad she had insisted on his coming along—the ten extra pounds were more than worth their weight.

Alan Michaels had told them he would meet them at the Hong Kong airport, adding that he'd gotten them special landing clearance, even though light planes ordinarily had to land twenty miles farther out. It was clear that Michaels had more clout in Hong Kong than he did in Calcutta—not surprising, since, according to Bobby, he had a huge manufacturing plant just outside the city.

Karen's bed was wheeled out and secured in the cargo bay, and Mira was given a seat right beside her. Charlie tried not to notice the fabrics that had been shoved against the back of the fuselage to make room for the large load. Nor could she allow herself to think about the Calcutta fabrics that had been unloaded and lugged away to some unknown storage facility prior to being shipped to Baltimore. *Remember,* she told herself severely, *you have no choice.* Karen's life hung in the balance, and that outweighed any other considerations.

They took off without difficulty, heading east across the Bay of Bengal. It was a clear afternoon, and they had a light tail wind that would work to their advantage, at least until they had to veer northward to avoid the restricted airspace over Laos and Vietnam. But Charlie noticed that Bobby kept a sharp eye on their altimeter. Despite the relative ease of the early part of their journey, he was still concerned about the extra weight on the plane.

They hadn't topped off their fuel tanks as they normally did on a journey of that length. *Electra* had a two-thousand-mile fuel range and, with the auxiliary tanks filled, they would have been able to fly straight through. But they needed every extra boost they could get, so they planned on a refueling stop in Mandalay before heading across the southern tip of China to Hong Kong. It seemed, as they glided in for a landing at the Mandalay

Airport, that they had judged correctly and that *Electra* could handle the extra weight without faltering. Charlie didn't bother to say to Bobby that this was further proof that their little jet was at the top of her class. Since no one else in the world was likely to hear about their rescue mission, it seemed pointless to discuss it.

It wasn't until they were out of Burmese airspace that the trouble began. Since they had only replaced enough fuel to get them to Hong Kong, the plane was no heavier than it had been when leaving Calcutta. But the wind had shifted, as it so often did over the Southeast Asian peninsula, and so they were battling a westerly flow that slowed them down.

That in itself would probably not have been enough to cause the problem, but the combination of the strong head wind and the additional weight seemed to strain even *Electra*'s sturdy reserves of strength. Halfway across the northern tip of Thailand, they began to feel the trouble.

Charlie had never dealt with an overload problem. *Electra*'s yoke suddenly felt stiff and resistant in her hand, and she had to fight for every inch of altitude. But it wasn't until they had crossed over into southern China— on the last leg of the journey—that the plane began to dangerously lose altitude.

And that was when Charlie finally lost control.

Up until that moment, ever since they had left Baltimore, she had felt she could handle any crisis that might come up during a flight. The bad weather during the Atlantic crossing, as well as the bird in the engine over India, had been difficult but not impossible for her to deal with. Now she was suddenly bereft of confidence in herself as a pilot. The control stick felt like a deadly enemy with a mind of its own. She blanked out on all the emergency measures she had learned so well at Jim Sullivan's insistence. The ground seemed to be coming up at her at an alarming rate, and she could no more stop the downward drop than she could control the sudden weakness in her knees or the faintness that threatened to overcome her at any moment.

She looked back into the cargo bay. Karen's stretcher bed appeared to be stable, and Karen herself was unaware of the new threat to her life. But Mira, sitting still and silent in the seat beside her patient, was pale and tight-lipped. *She must know,* Charlie thought. *She must know that her life is as endangered as Karen's.*

I have to do it, she decided, biting her lower lip so fiercely that a trickle of blood appeared, unnoticed, in the corner of her mouth. *I have to do it for Karen, if for no other reason.* She turned back, determined to make a superhuman effort to reverse the situation. But as she turned she caught sight of Bobby. He was sitting very straight in his seat, his hands on the copilot yoke, his eyes on the instrument panel before him. One look and Charlie knew he was as afraid as she was. When she thought that she might lose Bobby as well as her own life and those of her passengers, her last vestige of bravado was erased.

"Bobby," she whispered, her breath coming in quick, shallow gasps, "I can't do it. I . . . I can't keep her up in the air."

She turned a panicked face to him, her eyes blank and glistening with tears. She no longer cared that she was probably the only person aboard who could save *Electra*—the possibility of bringing the plane down for an emergency landing hadn't even occurred to her. She only knew that her mind and body had frozen in terror and that she was incapable of doing anything more than crying out blindly for help.

For a moment Bobby's face exactly mirrored her fears. He was as powerless as she was. They might as well have been two total novices rather than two experienced fliers, for all the presence of mind they possessed between them. Charlie had heard such stories before—perfectly good pilots with years of experience suddenly panicking and blanking out in the air. The only thing to do, a small part of her mind warned her, was to raise the nearest airport control tower on the radio and get a traffic controller to guide them down. But she couldn't even make her hands move toward the radio switch to give the Mayday signal. All she could do was sit there, facing Bobby, painfully aware of the two women who were doomed to go down with them through no fault of their own.

Charlie was sure that, given Bobby's innate fear of flying, he would be even less capable than she. But she had figured wrong. After that first moment of frozen panic, he seemed to come alive. He reached over and flicked on the radio switch and gave out the SOS call. Then he transferred the main control capability to his stick and began fighting once again to keep the careening plane on an even keel.

"Charlie," he said, his voice sounding like a stranger's, "get back in the cargo bay and start throwing things out. Open the little hatch window on the port side—that way there won't be such a sudden oxygen drain. I've switched on auxiliary oxygen—grab a mask." He turned back to Mira. "You grab one, too," he barked. "And get something rigged up over Karen's face. I don't think we're high enough to really need it, but it might help. Then help Miss Frehling toss things out."

Mira seemed to understand and reached up immediately to attach the oxygen masks that had dropped down from the top of the hold. Charlie was still immobilized in her seat.

"Did you hear me?" Bobby's eyes narrowed as he looked at Charlie's white face. "Charlie, I'm talking to you. Charlie!" Cursing softly, he risked taking one hand off the yoke in order to shake Charlie's shoulder. Still no response. He slapped her cheek hard, so that the sound resounded through the cabin. Charlie gasped and blinked.

"Bobby? Bobby, we're going down. We can't stay up. There's too much weight. Bobby..."

She blinked again as she realized what had just happened and put her hand to her cheek as the sting settled in. She didn't have to ask why he'd hit her.

He reached out again to caress the red spot. "Are you okay?" There was no time to wait for a response. He saw that Charlie was focusing and that she was more in control. "Get back there and start tossing," he said, all business once more. "Start with the luggage, then the extra seating in the rear of the fuselage."

"What about...?" She had already gotten up, but she paused.

"What about what?" He turned to her, challenge in his eyes. He knew what she was talking about.

"The fabric," she said softly. "What about the fabric?"

His mouth twitched slightly. "Don't throw the fabric out yet. I may be able to bring us out of this mess. Just get back there and help Mira. And make sure Karen is all right."

Then he turned back to his task, and Charlie could tell he wasn't going to discuss the matter further. He was in command now, not her. She was too grateful to question his authority, even though she knew the heavy bolts of fabric posed the biggest danger. She moved back into the cargo area, where Mira, tense but efficient, had already secured the oxygen mask on Karen's face, taking care not to disturb the tubes and wires already attached to her. That was Charlie's friend under all that plastic and metal, and the sight of Karen, as well as the knowledge that Bobby was in charge of the plane, gave her the strength to go on with what had to be done.

It took their combined efforts to open the small hatch, and when they did, the rush of air was tremendous. Fortunately they weren't up so high that oxygen depletion was a problem. Steeling themselves against the gale, Charlie and Mira set about stuffing whatever they could through the opening. Charlie could barely hear Bobby's voice over the roar of the wind, but she could tell he'd raised the nearest airport on the radio, and that he was getting instructions for a possible emergency landing on Macao. She glanced forward and saw him, sitting tense and urgent but clearly in control of the situation. What had happened to the frightened man who turned pale during every takeoff? He had found the strength to take control when she had lost the ability to act.

Charlie was grateful and relieved and was able to function again thanks to his command. She knew he was still afraid but had overcome his fears because he had no other choice. Part of her wished she'd been able to maintain control. But she was happier to see Bobby flying the plane than she would have thought possible, and she knew the love they had acknowledged back in Calcutta had, through his act of bravery, deepened immeasurably. Despite the fact that they were still in considerable danger, Charlie went about her task with a smile. The crisis, as far as she was concerned, had passed.

As it turned out she was right. Charlie and Mira had just ejected the first fabric carton when Bobby yelled back to say that *Electra* had stabilized, and that it looked as if they were going to make it to Hong Kong, after all. Charlie hugged Mira, hugged Karen's still form, then moved forward into the cockpit. Bobby turned to smile at her, an unmistakable look of triumph on his face. They both took deep breaths and grinned foolishly. Words would have been useless at that moment to express their relief, so Bobby reached for Charlie's hand and held it tightly while with his other hand he gripped the now steady yoke.

They sat for a moment in silence, holding hands tightly and looking out the window for the first signs of the Hong Kong airport. "I guess," said Bobby after a pause, "I should explain something to you now."

Charlie smiled and shook her head. "You don't have to explain anything," she said softly. "You just saved our lives."

"True." He flashed her a big grin. "But having accomplished that, I feel brave enough to say what I've been afraid to say ever since I came to work for you."

"What?" Despite her euphoria, Charlie felt a brief stab of apprehension. What was he going to tell her about? A prison record? A skeleton in his closet? A wife?

"You've never known much about my past," Bobby began, "because I was scared to death you wouldn't hire me if you knew. You see, I haven't had much long-term flight experience, Charlie."

Charlie shook her head. "Could've fooled me, the way you pulled *Electra* out of that drop."

"That's just it. I did try to fool you. You see, I'm a terrific flight mechanic—the best in the business—but I've never done much flying because ... I've always been scared to death to fly. It used to be much worse than it is now—than it was, rather. I used to black out as soon as we'd hit the runway. Any good mechanic has to be a pilot, so I had to be able to fly. But my fear was really getting in the way of my job."

"Why did you choose to be a flight technician in the first place? If you hated to fly, it seems you could have made a better career choice."

He smiled a bit thinly. "I never had a choice. Ever hear of Haddon Aviation?"

"Haddon? I don't think— Oh, yes, of course! The people who designed the computerized altimeters and all the other experimental equipment."

"It's not experimental anymore, but it was when I started working there." Bobby took a deep breath. "It used to be called Haddon-Dupree, Charlie."

"Haddon—Dupree? You mean ... ?"

He nodded. "My father. He owned fifty percent of the company—as a matter of fact, it was his expertise that made Haddon what it is today. He was a pretty old-fashioned guy, my dad. He always assumed I'd take over his half when he was ready to retire." Bobby broke off and looked grimly away from Charlie for a moment. "But of course that would never have worked out. I could build 'em, he said, but I couldn't fly 'em. And who ever heard of the president of an aviation company who was afraid to fly a plane?"

Charlie looked at his face, which was etched with sorry memories. "That's not so unusual," she said softly. "After all, you don't have to fly 'em to build 'em, especially if you own the company."

Bobby laughed. "Try telling that to my dad. He felt I was a disgrace to the family name—to the industry. He sold the company out to his partner seven years ago. I got the hint and took off. I've been working as a technician ever since, trying to work out my fear of flying."

"So you can go back into the family business."

"No, it's too late for that, and I never was much on being an executive type, anyway. But just . . . to prove to myself and my dad that I can do it. Mostly to myself— my father died three years ago."

Charlie was silent, knowing there was nothing she could say that would be as eloquent as Bobby's story. He had overcome a lifelong fear in order to save himself and those he loved. As they made their approach into the Hong Kong airport, she could tell by the way he handled *Electra* that his fear was a thing of the past. Yet his past would always be with him.

Bobby brought the plane down lightly on the runway without any visible effort, then taxied to the gate as instructed by the flight control tower. There on the runway stood two ambulances and a long black limousine. The man standing at the car, tall, pale and anxious, was obviously Alan Michaels.

As soon as *Electra*'s engines had stopped, the plane was mobbed by medical technicians and a mechanical crew. The Macao tower had probably radioed *Electra*'s predicament to Hong Kong, since everyone seemed to be prepared for the worst. Alan Michaels hovered near the cargo-bay door, waiting for a glimpse of his daughter and trying not to intervene in the activities of the staff he had obviously assembled himself. It wasn't until Karen was wheeled safely out of the plane, pronounced in stable condition by the doctor on hand and whisked into an ambulance that Mr. Michaels turned to Charlie and

Bobby, who had been standing relatively unnoticed at the wing of the little jet.

"Who's responsible for bringing that plane through?" he demanded gruffly.

"He is," replied Charlie promptly.

"She is," said Bobby at exactly the same moment.

Each pointing to the other, they exchanged glances and smiled. "It was a mutual effort, Mr. Michaels," Charlie said.

Alan Michaels looked at both of them and allowed himself the barest of smiles. "Looks like the two of you work pretty well together, eh?" He bent forward and impulsively hugged Charlie. "It's good to see you again, Charlotte. The last time I saw you, I believe, you were a gangly high school graduate, weren't you?" He held her away and shook his head, his gray eyes misting. "I'm glad you were there for my little girl when she needed you. Gladder than you'll ever know."

Charlie nodded. "I think I can guess. I'm glad I was there, too."

Karen's father turned to Bobby. "And you, young man." He held out his hand. "I guess you've come a long way since you left your father's business. According to the radio report from Macao, you were pretty impressive up there. Thanks."

Bobby grasped the hand and shook it, both acknowledgment and gratitude in his eyes. So, Charlie thought, Mr. Michaels had known who had brought *Electra* in, and he knew Bobby Dupree, too. Well, she was glad for Bobby—he deserved a pat on the shoulder. He deserved more, but that would have to wait until a more appropriate moment.

"I've got a limo waiting to take you wherever you want to go," Mr. Michaels said. "What'll it be?"

Again both Charlie and Bobby responded together. "The hospital." Mr. Michaels nodded gratefully. "I was hoping you'd say that. I want you to be there for Karen when she wakes up. Let's get you through customs quickly, and we'll be on our way."

Charlie found Alan Michaels's sturdy optimism encouraging. He seemed so capable and so able to get things done the way he wanted that she, too, began to feel more certain about Karen's recovery. They had started to walk to the customs station when Bobby remembered something.

"The General! I forgot to get the General!" He turned and ran back to the plane.

"The General?" Mr. Michaels was confused.

Charlie smiled. "Our mascot—a little mutt we picked up in Nice. The poor thing must have been terrorized by that flight. He'll be glad to get on solid land for a while, I'm sure."

That was an understatement. Bobby emerged from *Electra* with a bundle of fluffy white energy that could scarcely be contained. Bobby let him down on the tarmac for a few moments, then scooped him back up. "Okay," he said as he came over to the other two, "here we go again through customs. Let's see what penalty they have in store for us this time around, eh, General?"

"Have you had trouble with the dog?" Mr. Michaels inquired.

Bobby nodded. "He's had all his vaccinations, but apparently there are fairly strict quarantine laws in most ports of entry."

The other man's jaw set firmly. "Well. We'll just have to see about that." And taking a startled General Lee from Bobby's arms, he strode ahead of them into the customs shed.

"Do you think he's going to be able to do anything?" Charlie whispered to Bobby. "I mean, sometimes that kind of attitude can really backfire."

Bobby shrugged. "We'll see. He doesn't look like the kind of man who will take no for an answer—especially not in person." He grinned. "It looks like the General has faith in him, doesn't it?"

Indeed, all they could see of the General was his little tail, sticking out from under Alan Michaels's arm and wagging enthusiastically as if he knew he was in good hands. And he was right. By the time Bobby and Charlie got to the customs shed, everything appeared to have been settled. General Lee and their few remaining pieces of luggage had been passed through without inspection, and Charlie noticed one uniformed guard putting a folded wad of bills into his pocket. *Well*, she thought, *whatever works*.

Unfortunately they weren't so successful when they got out on the other side, where the ambulance and the limousine were now waiting. Next to the two cars was a crowd of reporters, and Charlie could tell by the way Mr. Michaels's face darkened that he hadn't reckoned on this kind of delay.

"How the hell did you guys get here?" he bellowed, but the press was not cowed.

"Mr. Michaels, you know you're news. And these pilots have made a dramatic rescue—they're heroes."

"We don't want to be heroes." Bobby glowered and took a threatening step toward one of the photographers.

"I'm afraid you have no choice," said the photographer, although he took a cautionary step backward. "You sacrificed that race you were in to save a friend's life— that's news, believe me."

Mr. Michaels was already herding them into the waiting Mercedes. "My daughter's life is still in danger," he barked at the press. "If you folks hold us up one second more, you'll have a lawsuit on your hands that you'll never be able to swallow—neither will your publishers."

Apparently that was a potent warning, because the crowd backed off and let them pass. At a gesture from Alan Michaels, the entourage pulled away from the curb and proceeded swiftly to the hospital. General Lee was the only one who bothered to look back.

10

KAREN BEGAN TO PULL OUT of her coma about six hours later, and within an hour after that she had recovered sufficiently to address her father with her usual dry humor. "Daddy," she said, "would you do me a big favor and fire Devon? He's a brute, you know."

In that moment Alan Michaels dropped his gruff manner. Tears filled his eyes as he sat, actually smiling with relief, on his daughter's bed. Despite the doctors' assurance that Karen probably would have pulled out of her coma in Calcutta, he remained convinced that only his quick thinking—and Charlie and Bobby's quick action—had saved his daughter's life. He had an image of the Calcutta hospital as a primitive operation and refused to be told otherwise. Charlie and Bobby, as relieved at Karen's recovery as they were, decided not to press the issue.

"Devon's already out, honey," Mr. Michaels told Karen, a fierce frown creasing his forehead at the mere thought of the man. "If he ever flies again, for anyone, I'll be very surprised."

Karen nodded and turned to Charlie, who was beaming at her from the foot of the bed. "I think that means Daddy's taken care of business," she explained unnecessarily. "And you know what *that* means—you don't mess around with Daddy."

"So we've learned," Charlie replied with a grin.

"Now," said Karen, "would somebody please tell me what's been going on? The last thing I remember was landing in Calcutta."

All the explanations—where she was, how she'd gotten there, how long she'd been in a coma—were undertaken, with numerous interruptions from the medical team, which constantly cautioned the patient and her visitors against too much excitement. But Karen, although pale, seemed to be rebounding with remarkable rapidity, and she waved away the overly solicitous nurses.

"Charlie...Bobby..." It was her turn to get misty with emotion. "How can I thank you for what you did?"

"You just did," said Bobby gently, taking her hand on one side of the bed while Charlie took the other. Mr. Michaels, having been assured his daughter would recover, was in a corner of the room on the telephone. He had already moved on to other matters of importance now that his daughter had been taken care of. "You've thanked us by getting well."

"I wouldn't have . . . without you." Karen turned from one to the other. "And don't think I don't know what it took for you to bring me here."

"Took?" Charlie tried to make light of the matter. "It took nothing. I've always said *Electra* could handle anything, and she did."

Karen shook her head. "You had to drop out of the race for this, didn't you?" Neither Charlie nor Bobby bothered to answer the rhetorical question. "That race meant a lot to you, and you gave it all up to bring me to Hong Kong."

Bobby shrugged. "I hear Manila's no fun, anyway."

"And we would never have gotten General Lee through customs there," Charlie added. But she and Bobby knew that Karen, of all people, understood the nature of their sacrifice and the extent of the danger they had endured on her behalf. All three were silent for a moment until Mr. Michaels got off the phone and turned back to them.

"Well," he said, rubbing his hands together in satisfaction, "I guess that's taken care of."

"Big business deal, Daddy?" Karen's voice was affectionate, but Charlie thought she detected a wistful note in it. Alan Michaels had certainly not spent much time on his daughter once the crisis had passed.

"Not very." He looked at Charlie and Bobby, standing like sentinels on either side of Karen's bed. "What are you two doing, posting guard?" He came over and edged Bobby out of position to take his daughter's hand. "Don't you both have something better to do?"

Charlie was confused and a little hurt. She had gone through too much to be dismissed so easily. She looked to Bobby for support, but he, after looking closely at Mr. Michaels, had gone to use the phone himself.

"Daddy," Karen began, embarrassment and annoyance in her voice. But Alan Michaels squeezed her hand to silence her.

"Don't 'Daddy' me," he said impatiently, then turned to Charlie. "Well, Charlotte, what have you got to say for yourself?"

"Say? I'm not sure I understand...." Charlie was fighting to control her own anger. He must have known she had nothing at all to do now that she had lost both the race and her access to manufacturing time at the Manila factory.

"It's very simple," he said rather smugly. "I just called the airport and had them get *Electra* refueled and ready for takeoff."

"Takeoff? But—"

"No buts. I believe you have a race to finish, don't you?"

"A race?" Charlie looked at Bobby, who had just gotten off the telephone, for help, but he had gone to stand beside Karen's father.

"Mr. Michaels," Bobby said, "I'm afraid we forfeited our chance in the race when we brought Karen here. I thought you understood that."

"And I thought *you* understood that Alan Michaels takes care of business," he retorted.

Karen, who had caught on, excitedly squeezed her father's hand. "Oh, Daddy," she whispered reverently, and the look in her father's eyes when he glanced down at her indicated he had just been amply repaid for his efforts.

"It seems Mr. Michaels has arranged for us to continue on in the race, Charlie. Is that right, sir?"

"Of course! You don't think I'd let a few silly rules and regulations get in our way, do you? That's not my style, and I can tell it's not yours, either."

Charlie shook her head, stunned by this revelation. "How on earth did you get them to agree to this? I mean, I wasn't exactly their favorite contestant to begin with."

Mr. Michaels chuckled. "I know. The head of the race committee told me you had been nothing but trouble right from the start." He looked positively gleeful at the thought. "Fortunately I have some clout with those idiots, and I made it very clear that if they didn't allow you to reenter, and didn't deduct the time it took you to take care of Karen, I would see to it that the international trade commission—which sponsors the race—would hear from me personally." He chuckled again. "I also mentioned that, seeing as you two seem to be media stars and all that, that it wouldn't look very good if word got out that you had been disqualified. The press, you see, is good for something, after all."

Charlie was still shaking her head, although a big smile now lit up her face. "I don't believe it." She turned to Bobby. "Do you?"

He nodded emphatically. "Sure I do. I know how this guy operates." He reached out and clapped Alan Michaels heartily on the shoulder. "He reminds me of another aeronautics magnate I once knew. A prince of a man, just like my father."

"That's quite a compliment, son," said Alan Michaels with unaccustomed humility. "He was a terrific guy. And his son takes after him, I can see that now."

The two men allowed themselves a moment's mutual gratitude before Bobby turned back to Charlie. "Well, Chief, I guess we'd better hit the road, wouldn't you say? We've got some fancy flying to do to catch up to the rat pack."

Charlie looked at Karen. "Get out of here," Karen said softly.

"Are you sure you'll be okay?"

Karen rolled her eyes dramatically. "Okay? With the fabulous Alan Michaels here to supervise my recovery?" She smiled at her father and then turned back to Charlie. "I don't have any choice in the matter. Besides," she added gently. "I'd never forgive myself if you didn't get back in there and give it another try. For me."

"Forgive yourself?" Alan Michaels sounded appalled. "I'd never forgive *her*! Now, Charlotte," he went on sternly, "you owe it to yourself and to your reputation as a rebel to go back in there and prove that nobody pushes Charlotte Frehling around, do you hear?"

Charlie giggled at the fatherly command. "Yes, sir," she replied, saluting smartly. "Ready, copilot Dupree?"

"You bet!"

While Charlie was saying goodbye to Karen, Bobby and Mr. Michaels held a hasty conference. On the way out of the hospital Charlie asked him what it had been about, but he told her an explanation would have to wait until they were airborne.

The press made sure of that. Having been given the all-clear by one of Alan Michaels's silent minions, journalists descended on the couple like vultures, plying them with questions and waving cameras in their faces with no apparent regard for either their hurry or their safety. Once again Bobby had to physically hold them at bay while he and Charlie were whisked into the Michaels's Mercedes and off to the airport.

The harassment didn't stop there, either. Charlie couldn't tell if this was a new batch of press hounds or if the others had managed by superhuman means to beat the limo to the airport. But there they were, shouting questions about Bobby and Charlie's dangerous flight from Calcutta and current flight plans. They also asked about the pilots' individual pasts—they had apparently done their homework in *that* department—and, of course, about the couple's romantic involvement.

Charlie was glad to let Bobby handle the press while she hastily filed the flight plan. He was good at talking to reporters, blending judicious information with smart retorts that kept the media people smiling and scribbling. By the time he and Charlie were ready to board, he had turned the attitude from voracious inquisitiveness to a friendly curiosity.

"You're a natural at public relations," Charlie told him as they taxied to their takeoff position. She noticed that Bobby displayed none of the anxiety that he had on former takeoffs. He was relaxed and happy as he fiddled with dials and surveyed their charts.

"It's surprising to find out how much comes naturally to me lately," he said with a smile, and she knew he was pleased with his newfound ease in the air. "I have you to thank for that, Charlie."

They had taken off and were banking southeast over Tathong Channel for the short hop across the South China Sea to the Philippines. "That's not true. You have only yourself to thank, Bobby."

He shook his head, squinting out across the blue glare of the sunny afternoon. "I wouldn't have been able to overcome my fear if I hadn't had you to think about, you know. That's what made me go into action. It was that or risk losing you forever. Losing your respect, if not your very life." He shuddered involuntarily. "I couldn't let that happen."

"I understand." As if by some prearranged signal, their hands inched out and met in the small space between their seats. "It's like once you have something to live for, living becomes more urgent."

"Exactly. And we have everything to live for. This race, your business . . . and, of course, us."

Charlie knew he was speaking from his heart, as she was, but that mention of her business reminded her that she had lost an important deal, and that the Electra shops would suffer severely for that loss. Having forfeited her place in the factory's production schedule, she would have to go to the end of the line and now, with everyone's winter production in full swing, she would never get her sportswear out in time to compete with the other houses. The fabric she had shipped from the various cities would arrive, all right, but without Charlie's samples the factory had nothing to go by. Deadlines, in this business, were sacrosanct. It would be useless to argue with the production manager once she got to Manila. Money was money, and there was plenty to be made without Charlie Frehling's relatively small order.

Still, she didn't want to say anything to Bobby. Too much had gone right for her to mar their current happiness. It was just a small professional setback that Charlie would have to absorb.

Bobby was perceptive and persistent, however; he noticed her momentary musing. "We *do* have everything to live for, Charlie," he repeated. "Don't you agree?"

She turned and gave him a half-hearted smile. "We have each other, and that's what matters," she hedged. "And Karen is going to be all right, and—"

"Forget about Karen, and us. I'm talking about you." He sounded severe, but there was a sparkle in his eyes that she didn't understand. "Don't you have everything to live for?"

"Of course I do."

"Except one thing, right?"

"No," she said carefully. "I have everything I could possibly want."

"Bull! Come on, Charlie, admit it, won't you? You feel lousy about the loss of that factory time, don't you? Don't you?"

"Well . . ." She wondered why he was being so adamant. She herself would have preferred to forget all about it—to write it off as a loss and go on. "It's really not that big a deal, Bobby. I've survived worse setbacks with the Electra shops, you know."

"But you feel lousy about this one, and you don't want to admit it because you think it will make me feel bad, don't you?"

His pointed honesty was unassailable. "There's nothing much we can do about it," she said curtly, "so why bother to bring it up?"

"Oh, come on now. That doesn't sound like the Charlie Frehling I know! The Charlie I know doesn't take anything lying down, no matter how happy she is. She's a fighter and a winner. Aren't you? Well, aren't you?"

"Of course I am!" He was goading her to real impatience. "But I just don't see—" She broke off as she finally realized the meaning of that twinkle in his eyes. Her eyes narrowed. "Bobby, do you know something I don't know?"

He chuckled, but seemed to enjoy stringing her along. "Would that bother you? To have me know something you don't?" He was clearly playing with her.

"Tell me!"

"Okay," he relented easily. "When I heard Alan Michaels wheeling and dealing on the phone, I realized I could play the same game. I called the factory in Manila and told them to hold your deadline for forty-eight hours, that something had come up and that we would gladly pay for the holdup if they would wait."

"You told them that? But why would they have agreed to that? They have no reason to listen to you."

He chuckled again. "They do if they think I'm the editor of *Fashion World*."

"*Fashion World*? But they're the biggest trade publication in the industry!" She was horrified. "How could you lie like that? Surely they'll find you out!"

Bobby shook his head. "I worked it all out with Michaels. Naturally he knows someone who knows someone on the magazine's editorial board who owes him a favor. And naturally he agreed to make a quick phone call to ensure that my story will be verified."

"But...that's crazy! How did you ever think you could get away with it?"

"How did you think you could ever get away with telling the FAI officials you were using dog fur for your winter line?" he demanded. Charlie stared at him for a moment, recognized the outrageousness of what she had done and burst into laughter.

"You're absolutely right," she said. "One crazy story deserves another." Then she grew serious again. "But I left all that fabric behind in Calcutta. All those beautiful silks!"

"Not to worry. Alan Michaels sent the Gulfstream back to pick it up before it could be shipped to Baltimore. It should arrive in Manila the same time we do."

She looked at him and shook her head in disbelief. "You know something?" she said softly. "You are the most amazing thing that's ever happened to me."

"Ditto for me," he said, "let's set this baby down in Manila and take care of business." His eyes smoldered briefly. "I mean, first we'll take care of business, and then we'll take care of business."

Charlie knew exactly what he meant.

IF CHARLIE AND BOBBY thought their departure from Hong Kong was embellished by hoopla, they were stunned by the reception they got in Manila. Reporters crowded around *Electra* almost before she had pulled to a full stop in front of the terminal. They were joined by a group of FAI officials, who had obviously been ordered to put on a show of welcoming the rebel fliers back into the fold. And numerous hangers-on were there only because they'd seen the crowd.

The questions fired at the two pilots were more intense this time as details of Charlie and Bobby's life became fodder for the media mill. *Flying* magazine wanted to do a profile on Bobby Dupree and Karen Michaels, children of the "aeromagnates," as they were called. *Cosmopolitan* wanted to do a piece on women fliers—how to look terrific at twelve thousand feet. *People* wanted to cover the human-interest angle, both the adventure and the romance. And *Fashion World*, having received their mysterious orders from on high, proposed a big profile on Charlie, following her rise to fame as a designer right through to her negotiations with the factory in Manila for what *Fashion World* was already dubbing, "the sportswear line that saved a life."

Charlie was fairly disgusted with the hullabaloo, but Bobby, playing his new wheeler-dealer role to the hilt, gave as much information as he could without actually slowing his stride from the plane to the customs shed to the limousine that awaited them. Charlie loved the way he played with words, the way he left the reporters feeling he had given them a special tidbit, when all he had said was what had been said before.

She herself was having trouble believing it had all come true so fast—Karen's recovery, their requalification in the race and the salvation of her winter line. The combined strain, excitement and constant pressure from the crowd made her feel slightly dizzy and out of her element. She felt ill-prepared for the bout of bargaining she would have to endure at the factory and couldn't get her thoughts together about what fabrics she wanted with which designs. She needed more time, time to sort through her purchases, to rethink her last-minute decisions about designs, time just to sleep and catch up on herself. But time was the one thing Alan Michaels hadn't been able to arrange for them. He had bought them a place back on the roller coaster, and it was up to them to go the distance on their own energy and wits.

Charlie looked at Bobby—he seemed to be thriving under the pressure, just as she had expected she would herself. But all she really wanted to do was go off somewhere and be with him, to recapture that first thrill of love and discover each other at their leisure, rather than always having to rush off to some assignment with destiny. This was the first time in her life that she had felt this way about a man. Charlie resented not being able to play out the wealth of emotions she held in her heart for Bobby, even though she knew it was her own interests that kept her from doing so.

Their love affair would have to wait until other business was taken care of, although Charlie rated Bobby at least as high in importance as the Electra boutiques. Higher, really, since she had had the shops for many years and she had just discovered Bobby. He was now paramount in her life. But she didn't want to rob him of the thrill of competition, for she knew he had something very special to prove to the world as Bobby Dupree, formerly of Haddon-Dupree Aviation. And she would never have jeopardized the future of the Electra shops and their staff for her own private interests.

So she went along with the game plan, even though her heart wasn't in it. She allowed herself to be whisked away to the factory while Bobby stayed behind to supervise the unloading of the fabric from the Calcutta shipment and to take care of General Lee. Somehow her innate skills as a designer, businesswoman and bargainer came to her aid, for she was soon immersed in the round of discussions that would put her winter line into production. The factory managers, having been given the word that this was indeed a prestigious account, and very much aware of the publicity surrounding their attractive client, went out of their way to be accommodating. Still it took most of the day before design patterns, production procedures, prices and finish deadlines were agreed on.

Bobby had arrived at some point with the rest of the material; his presence seemed to give Charlie the extra energy she needed to get through the ordeal. But by the time the final handshake had been repeated for the press photographers, she was bone weary and barely able to stand up. She hoped they wouldn't have to leave that night on the next leg of their journey. As a matter of fact, she had every intention of refusing to budge without at least eight hours' sleep under her belt. The next major stop was Hawaii, 4,600 miles away, which would mean a minimum of two full days' flying, including pit stops.

Bobby, as it turned out, had no intention of leaving right away. He had reserved a room for them in the Royal Philippines Hotel—the honeymoon suite, he confided, and suddenly Charlie wasn't quite as tired as she had been.

"I'm sick of running around hotel corridors—and balconies—and sneaking a few hours with you on a narrow hospital bed. I want to start our life together the right way—really together, and I don't care if that's news to the press. If they haven't figured our story out already, they're pretty slow on the uptake."

This speech was delivered in the limousine on the way to the hotel, and Charlie, peering through the back window at the inevitable taxi filled with reporters, had to laugh. "I think they'd be delighted. Imagine the great copy we'll make: Lifesaving Pilots Book Room Together for Love Tryst! That'll go over real well!"

Bobby rolled his eyes wickedly. "Especially when they see how I've registered. That'll really send them. I just hope they'll stay out of our hair for at least the night."

"How did you register?"

"As Mr. and Mrs. Dupree, of course."

To her surprise, Charlie found herself blushing. "What do you think they'll do when they find out we're phonies?"

Bobby's grin softened. "It doesn't have to be a phony," he said, lifting her hand to his lips. "We can stop off at a justice of the peace—or whatever they're called locally—and remedy that right away, if you like."

Charlie tried to hide her reaction by making light of the situation. "Why, Bobby Dupree," she drawled, "is that a proposal I'm hearing from you?"

"You know it is." He was totally serious. She could feel his heart beating as he pressed her palm to his chest. "It shouldn't come as any surprise to you—not after Caracas and Cairo, not after Nice, and especially not after Calcutta. You mean more to me than anything else in the world, Charlie, and I'll marry you the minute you say the word, no matter when or where."

Charlie swallowed back tears and leaned forward to gently kiss him. "I accept," she whispered against his throat. "But we don't have time to get married right now. We've got a race to run tomorrow." She pulled away and ran a finger around his lips. "A night with you in the honeymoon suite will suit me just fine for now, darling."

"You mean it?"

"Of course I mean it. There's nothing I'd like better."

"No, I mean about getting married."

Charlie was actually surprised to hear him pursue it. He should know how she felt. "Bobby, I'd marry you in a minute, too. But we do have the race to finish—"

"To hell with the race!"

This time she was shocked. "Are you kidding? I thought..."

"You thought it was more important to me than you? Are you kidding?" His eyes narrowed. "How about you, Charlie? Is the race that important to you that you feel we have to finish it?"

Charlie had no time to collect her thoughts on the subject. "No, I just thought...Alan Michaels went through a lot to get us back in the lineup, and..." She looked at Bobby, who returned her gaze with a challenge in his eyes. "I thought it mattered a lot to you, Bobby. Because of your father and because of overcoming your fears and wanting the world to know."

"You think that's more important to me than having the world know about us? I love you, Charlie. That's what's transformed my life, not some silly race around the world. I want us to start our life together now—not wait until we've exhausted ourselves trying to prove we can keep up with the big guys." His voice softened. "I thought it was you who needed to stay in the race, so that you could prove that a woman could do it."

She smiled. "Frankly, my dear," she said in the heaviest drawl she could muster, "I don't give a damn, either. All I care about is you."

They slid together along the seat until their bodies melted into one. Suddenly everything else was unimportant except that they were together and that they both felt the same way about each other. *This* was what counted most. Their lips sealed their words with a promise of commitment and passion. Charlie, freed from the constraints that the upcoming flight had placed on her, felt as if she had just been given a new lease on life. Every nerve and muscle in her body responded with a surge of energy that traveled like electricity through her body to Bobby's and then back to hers, recharged by his equal and opposite force. For all her independence and his, they were at that moment two interlocking parts of a whole. Separate and following their own destinies, they were weak and fatigued, but together they made up more than the sum of their parts. They were invincible.

"So!" said Bobby, pulling away and rubbing his hands together eagerly. "We get married. But when? And where?"

"The sooner the better."

"Well, we could find the appropriate official here in Manila and take care of it right away, as I said before." He peered out the window as if expecting to see a justice of the peace office appear in front of his eyes. "After all, we've got the honeymoon suite reserved already...."

Charlie looked out her side of the car window. This section of Manila wasn't particularly appealing, filled with shoddy storefronts and high rises that made it look like any one of a hundred cities in the world.

Bobby seemed to have read her thoughts. "But this doesn't strike you as the most romantic place in the world to get hitched, does it?"

Charlie giggled. "The only thing I can think of in connection with Manila is the Ali-Frazier fight a decade or so ago—the 'thrilla in Manila,' I think it was called."

Bobby made a face. "Ugh! Not exactly a precedent for the wedding of the century, is it?" He leaned over and kissed her nose, reaching out and winding her long hair around his palm in what had become a characteristic gesture of affection. "Besides, if we get married here everyone will be breathing down our necks for us to get on with the race. I'm sure the press would love it if we spent our honeymoon flying *Electra* to Hawaii and points east—personally, I have other things in mind for us." He drew her hair across her throat in a seductive motion that made Charlie sigh.

"I can think of a better place to be than in *Electra*, too, much as I love that plane."

"Like where?"

"Where?" Charlie leaned back against his arm and closed her eyes, allowing her mind to wander lazily across the map of the world she had come to know so well. "Well, I don't know, someplace exotic and out of the way. Someplace outrageously quiet but decadent." She thought for a moment. "Like Bora Bora, maybe, or Zanzibar or Tahiti...."

"Hmm..." Bobby seemed to be taking her daydreams seriously. Suddenly he sat bolt upright. "Tahiti! Of course!"

Charlie's eyes flew open. "Tahiti? What do you mean, 'of course'?"

"I mean, Tahiti is the perfect place. It's accessible from here, but it's remote. It's private but lush and exotic. You can't get more exotic than Tahiti." He leaned back and grinned. "And isn't that where the men of the *Bounty* stopped when they mutinied?" He wiggled his eyebrows mischievously.

Charlie stared at him for a moment before grinning back. "And you plan to mutiny, is that it?"

"Only if my captain comes along with me," he replied, pressing his lips against her neck in a way that was guaranteed to raise her temperature. "Of course, if you don't agree, I'll simply have to kidnap you."

"Hah! That *is* mutiny!"

He planted a last teasing kiss on the clothed tip of her breast, but the effect was so arousing that it felt as if he had caressed her bare nipple. "They don't call me a rebel for nothing, you know," he drawled deeply, and Charlie let her breath out in a shudder of desire. "Well, Captain, what'll it be? Either you mutiny with me, or you come as my prisoner. Either way," he added, twirling an imaginary mustache, "I'll have my way with you before the day is out. You'll be my wife, wench, whether you like it or not."

Charlie laughed huskily, took his face in her hands and kissed him, hard and deep, on the mouth. "No one," she said when she pulled away to let him catch his breath, "outrebels Charlie Frehling." She turned to the driver, who was attempting to ignore what was going on in his backseat. "Driver. Take us to the airport instead of the hotel, please."

If they had been reenacting a romantic thriller, they couldn't have asked for a more obliging chauffeur. With an impressive skidding and screeching of tires, the man executed a perfect U-turn in the middle of a busy street, leaving the two cars full of reporters floundering in the midst of a horrendous traffic jam. Then he sped off in the opposite direction, ignoring red lights and irate motorists.

They pulled up in front of the private plane terminal in record time. Then Charlie and Bobby went into action. Charlie filed a flight plan, shelling out several large bills to ensure that the plan wasn't made public until well after their departure. Bobby went to rescue the General, who was beginning to think life was a series of such adventures and who appeared to have adapted quite well to the excitement.

Luck was with them, for they managed to get an almost immediate departure time. *Electra*, having been thoroughly serviced under Bobby's watchful eye, and obviously feeling chipper without her extra cargo load, seemed to fly by herself through the sapphire skies. They crossed the Philippine Sea into the Pacific Islands, then stopped on one of the Solomons to refuel, and again in American Samoa. Somewhere along the way they took time out to sleep. But it wasn't until late the next day, when they arrived in Tahiti, that Bobby and Charlie allowed themselves to stop.

They had rented a cottage-like hut right on the western shore of the island, as far away from the main town as they could get. General Lee was with them, since Tahiti seemed to have no qualms about letting a perfectly healthy dog into its domain. The palm trees rustled over the small porch where they sat. The sweet smell of the breadfruit and citrus trees would have been overpowering if not for the salty ocean tang borne in on the light wind. It was quite late in the day, and the sky had blossomed into outrageous pinks and purples in preparation for the glorious sunset.

Bobby and Charlie sat together on a bamboo swing, letting the weight of their bodies carry them slowly back and forth. They were examining a small piece of white paper, holding it between them as if it were a talisman.

"Well, Mrs. Dupree," Bobby said quietly, "that wasn't too difficult, now was it?"

"Mr. Dupree, it was a snap. Of course, having just the person we needed at the airport helped things along, didn't it?" She smiled at him. "But I would have gone through hell and high water with you to get this piece of paper, Bobby, so it really doesn't matter."

"Really? You don't care about not having a big wedding? A big celebration?"

In answer she pressed her body more tightly along his, so that the swing rocked violently forward. "I intend to

have a big celebration, Mr. Dupree," she drawled. "But
the only ones I'm inviting are you and me."

Bobby caught her lower lip and held it for a moment
between his teeth. "What? Not even the General?" He
reached out and touched the fluffy dog reclining at their
feet. "Did you hear that, General? You're not invited."
Bobby's voice sounded petulant, as he meant it to, but
his hands were doing things to Charlie's hips and thighs
that belied that emotion.

"Actually," Charlie whispered hoarsely against his ear,
"I was hoping the General would stand guard duty for
us. After all, big celebrations are no fun if they get interrupted. And we have no idea how close on our tail the
rest of the world may be."

"Oh, I wouldn't worry about that," said Bobby, pro-
ceeding to unbutton Charlie's shirt while he spoke. "After
all, we greased enough palms to make a clean getaway.
The only person who's liable to figure things out is Alan
Michaels. And I have an idea he'll do his best to leave well
enough alone."

Charlie giggled, more from the touch of his fingers
against her nipples than from the thought of all those
people scratching their heads in confusion about their
sudden disappearance. "I wish I could see the expression on the face of that FAI official. After all that effort
to get us back in the race, he finds out we've cut loose
again—Oh . . . that feels nice." Bobby had removed her
top and was tracing tiny curlicues along her breasts with
his tongue. "I'm glad we thought to cable Marla, though.
I wouldn't have wanted her to think . . . oh, Bobby!"

Bobby had slipped down to his knees beside the swing
and was burying his head in Charlie's lap, working his
lips and his hands into the elastic waist of the white silk
harem pants she had put on as a bridal gesture. She

leaned back against the seat to give him easier access, thrusting her fingers urgently into his thick hair and feeling the fire he was building in her loins spread through her entire body. The warm breeze preserved the heat in her bare breasts, and she could feel the temperature rising as Bobby slipped the light silk down her legs.

"This is what I was hoping you would buy in Calcutta for me," he murmured, his lips following the trail of silk. "Something incredibly soft and sensuous . . . something perfect for taking off. God, you're lovely. You're lovely, and you're my wife."

He stood up, and Charlie gently undid his trousers and shirt until he, too, stood naked and ready before her. When they could no longer stand the strain of being apart, he reached down and scooped her up in his arms as if she weighed no more than General Lee.

"General," he said stepping over the dozing mutt on the way into the hut, "you've been assigned first-mate duties. We don't want to be disturbed for at least . . ." He smiled down at Charlie. "At least four or five days. Is that clear?"

He stepped through the door and kicked it shut behind him. And soon neither Charlie nor Bobby were in a position to hear as the General scooted over to lie directly in front of the door. Nor did they hear his quiet bark, which sounded very much like a salute.

Spoil yourself next month
with these four novels from

— TEMPTATION —

THE HOOD by Carin Rafferty

Meet Matt Cutter — another in Temptation's sinfully sexy
line-up of men under the banner *Rebels & Rogues*. Matt was a
street-wise rebel who had never thought to hear of Doria
Sinclair again. As a teenager, he had taken the rap for one of
her crimes, and now that she had walked back into his life, he
swore he wouldn't be taken in by her again . . .

A DARK AND STORMY KNIGHT by Tiffany White

Nicholas Knight was trying to run Ali Charbonneau out of
town, but she knew he would like nothing better than to keep
her in his bed. Ali stirred up painful memories and he didn't
want a repeat of bad history. The townspeople thought he had
murdered the woman he had loved. And, sometimes, Nicholas
did, too . . .

AT LONG LAST LOVE by Gina Wilkins
The final story in her *Veils & Vows* wedding trilogy

Neal Archer was looking forward to leading the life of a
carefree bachelor now that his daughter was newlywed. Now
he would have the chance to get to know sexy photographer
Holly Baldwin much, much better, but she was unlike any of
the women he usually dated . . .

HEARTTHROB by Janice Kaiser

Sydney Charles was desperate. She was a private investigator
with no money coming in and then she heard that actor Zinn
Garrett and his young daughter needed protection from a
crazed female fan who was stalking them. How easy would it
be to convince Zinn to hire her to pose as his live-in lover to
bait the trap?

SPRING IS IN THE AIR . . .

AND SO IS ROMANCE

Springtime Romance – A collection of stories
from four popular Mills & Boon authors, which
we know you will enjoy this Springtime.

GENTLE SAVAGE	–	Helen Brooks
SNOWDROPS FOR A BRIDE	–	Grace Green
POSEIDON'S DAUGHTER	–	Jessica Hart
EXTREME PROVOCATION	–	Sarah Holland

Available April 1993   Price £6.80